The Adventures of Tom Bombadil

Works by J.R.R. Tolkien

THE HOBBIT
LEAF BY NIGGLE
ON FAIRY-STORIES
FARMER GILES OF HAM
THE HOMECOMING OF BEORHTNOTH
THE LORD OF THE RINGS
THE ADVENTURES OF TOM BOMBADIL
THE ROAD GOES EVER ON (WITH DONALD SWANN)
SMITH OF WOOTTON MAJOR

Works published posthumously

SIR GAWAIN AND THE GREEN KNIGHT, PEARL AND SIR ORFEO*
THE FATHER CHRISTMAS LETTERS
THE SILMARILLION*
PICTURES BY J.R.R. TOLKIEN*
UNFINISHED TALES*
THE LETTERS OF J.R.R. TOLKIEN*
FINN AND HENGEST
MR BLISS
THE MONSTERS AND THE CRITICS & OTHER ESSAYS*
ROVERANDOM
THE CHILDREN OF HÚRIN*
THE LEGEND OF SIGURD AND GUDRÚN*
THE FALL OF ARTHUR*
BEOWULF: A TRANSLATION AND COMMENTARY*
THE STORY OF KULLERVO
THE LAY OF AOTROU AND ITROUN
BEREN AND LÚTHIEN*
THE FALL OF GONDOLIN*
THE NATURE OF MIDDLE-EARTH
THE FALL OF NÚMENOR

The History of Middle-earth – by Christopher Tolkien

I THE BOOK OF LOST TALES, PART ONE
II THE BOOK OF LOST TALES, PART TWO
III THE LAYS OF BELERIAND
IV THE SHAPING OF MIDDLE-EARTH
V THE LOST ROAD AND OTHER WRITINGS
VI THE RETURN OF THE SHADOW
VII THE TREASON OF ISENGARD
VIII THE WAR OF THE RING
IX SAURON DEFEATED
X MORGOTH'S RING
XI THE WAR OF THE JEWELS
XII THE PEOPLES OF MIDDLE-EARTH

* Edited by Christopher Tolkien

J.R.R. TOLKIEN

THE ADVENTURES OF TOM BOMBADIL

and other verses
from The Red Book

WITH ILLUSTRATIONS BY
PAULINE BAYNES

EDITED BY CHRISTINA SCULL
& WAYNE G. HAMMOND

WILLIAM MORROW
An Imprint of HarperCollinsPublishers

First published by George Allen & Unwin 1962
This edition first published by HarperCollins*Publishers* 2014
Copyright © The Tolkien Estate Limited 1962, 2014
Illustrations © HarperCollins*Publishers* 1962
Further copyright notices appear on page 301

🌣® and "Tolkien" ® are registered trademarks
of The J.R.R. Tolkien Estate Limited

HarperCollins books may be purchased for educational, business,
or sales promotional use. For information, please email the
Special Markets Department at SPsales@harpercollins.com.

First William Morrow paperback published 2024.

www.tolkienestate.com
www.tolkien.co.uk

Library of Congress Cataloging-in-Publication Data has been applied for.

ISBN 978-0-06-341354-2

24 25 26 27 28 LBC 5 4 3 2 1

CONTENTS

Agatha Christie

The Secret Adversary

A Tommy and Tuppence Mystery

_wm_

WILLIAM MORROW
An Imprint of HarperCollins_Publishers_

FIRST WILLIAM MORROW TRADE PAPERBACK PUBLISHED 2012.
FIRST WILLIAM MORROW TV TIE-IN EDITION PUBLISHED 2015.
SECOND WILLIAM MORROW PAPERBACK EDITION PUBLISHED 2020.
THIRD WILLIAM MORROW PAPERBACK EDITION PUBLISHED 2024.

Designed by Michael P. Correy

Library of Congress Cataloging-in-Publication Data has been applied for.

ISBN 978-0-06-339789-7

24 25 26 27 28 LBC 5 4 3 2 1

INTRODUCTION

In the first part of *The Lord of the Rings*, Frodo, Sam, Merry, and Pippin are crossing the Old Forest when they are attacked by the malevolent Old Man Willow. By good fortune, they are rescued by Tom Bombadil, 'a man, or so it seemed', singing nonsense and wearing 'an old battered hat with a tall crown and a long blue feather stuck in the band' and 'stumping along with great yellow boots on his thick legs. . . . He had a blue coat and a long brown beard; his eyes were blue and bright, and his face was red as a ripe apple, but creased into a hundred wrinkles of laughter' (bk. I, ch. 6). To the hobbits he is a saviour but a puzzle. When Frodo asks Goldberry, 'who is Tom Bombadil?' she replies simply, 'He is' – he, who at that moment is tending the hobbits' ponies and can be heard singing

Old Tom Bombadil is a merry fellow;
Bright blue his jacket is, and his boots are yellow.

At this, Frodo looks at Goldberry 'questioningly', and she adds: 'He is, as you have seen him. He is the Master of wood, water, and hill.' Later, when Frodo asks Tom himself, 'Who are you, Master?' the reply is: 'Don't you know my name yet? That's the only answer.' But he too elaborates, referring to the wider mythology, or 'matter of Middle-earth', which underlies *The Lord of the Rings*: 'Tom was here before the river and the trees; Tom remembers the first raindrop and the first acorn. He made paths before the Big People [Men and Elves], and saw the little People [Hobbits] arriving. He was here before the Kings and the graves and the Barrow-wights. When the Elves passed westward, Tom was here already, before the seas were bent' (bk. I, ch. 7).

One reader of *The Lord of the Rings*, Peter Hastings, felt that Goldberry's 'He is' implied that Tom Bombadil is God. Tolkien disagreed: 'Goldberry and Tom are referring to the mystery of *names*. . . . Frodo has asked not "what is Tom Bombadil" but "Who is he". We and he no doubt often laxly confuse the questions. Goldberry gives what I think is the correct answer. We need not go into the sublimities of "I am that am" [God's words to Moses in Exodus 3:14] – which is quite different from *he is*. She adds as a concession a statement of part of the "what"' (*Letters of J.R.R. Tolkien* (1981), pp. 191–2). Tolkien's readers have advanced many theories about Tom, without consensus; we have touched upon these in *The Lord of the Rings: A Reader's Companion* (2005), and will not rehearse them here. Although one learns more about Tom Bombadil as *The Lord of the Rings* continues, in the end he does not fit neatly into any category. He does not clearly belong to any one of the groups of intelligent beings established in Tolkien's private mythology, which also encompasses *The Hobbit* and the 'legends' of earlier days broadly referred to as 'The Silmarillion'. Nor could there be a definite answer to the question Who (or What) is Tom Bombadil, when his creator did not have one himself. To one reader, Tolkien said that he did not know Tom's origin, though he could make 'guesses', if he chose to do so, but preferred to leave Tom a mystery. To another, he commented that some things in the world of *The Lord of the Rings* should remain unexplained: 'even in a mythical Age there must be some enigmas, as there always are. Tom Bombadil is one (intentionally)' (*Letters*, p. 174). And to Peter Hastings, he wrote: 'I don't think Tom needs philosophizing about, and is not improved by it. But many have found him an odd or indeed discordant ingredient' (*Letters*, p. 192).

This last point can be explained by the fact that Tom

Bombadil existed in fiction before *The Lord of the Rings* was conceived. His name was given first to a 'Dutch doll' – a toy made of jointed wooden pegs – owned by one or more of Tolkien's children and dressed exactly as Tom is described in *The Lord of the Rings*; and as Tolkien did with other toys in his household, such as the little lead dog that inspired *Roverandom* and the teddy bears that appear in *Mr. Bliss*, he put Tom Bombadil into stories. A tantalizing fragment of one of these survives in the Bodleian Library at the University of Oxford, and is printed in the present book as an appendix.

Around 1931, Tolkien also put Tom into a poem. In this he created not only the now familiar Tom Bombadil, but also Goldberry, Old Man Willow, and the Barrow-wight, all of whom would figure in *The Lord of the Rings*. The poem was published as *The Adventures of Tom Bombadil* in the *Oxford Magazine* for 15 February 1934, and is reprinted below. Late in 1937, Tolkien brought the work to mind again when, his recently published *Hobbit* having proved a success, he was asked for a sequel, but at first was unable to think of one. Instead, he wrote to his publisher: 'Perhaps a new (if similar) line? Do you think Tom Bombadil, the spirit of the (vanishing) Oxford and Berkshire countryside [the country near Tolkien's home for most of his adult life], could be made into the hero of a story? Or is he, as I suspect, fully enshrined in the enclosed verses [from the *Oxford Magazine*]? Still I could enlarge the portrait' (*Letters*, p. 26). In the event, Tolkien focused his new story upon hobbits, but included Tom early on, as he wrote to Peter Hastings, 'because I had already "invented" him independently ... and wanted an "adventure" on the way' (*Letters*, p. 192). His 'portrait' of Tom in *The Lord of the Rings* was indeed an enlargement, but also a transformation, to suit a story which, like Tom himself, grew in the telling and became notably complex.

The character of Tom Bombadil appealed to Tolkien's Aunt Jane Neave, who asked him near the beginning of October 1961 if he 'wouldn't get out a small book with Tom Bombadil at the heart of it, the sort of size of book that we old 'uns can afford to buy for Christmas presents' (quoted in Humphrey Carpenter, *J.R.R. Tolkien: A Biography* (1977), p. 244). Tolkien replied that he thought Jane's request 'a good one, not that I feel inclined to write any more about [Tom]. But I think that the original poem (which appeared in the *Oxford Magazine* long before *The Lord of the Rings*) might make a pretty booklet of the kind you would like if each verse could be illustrated by Pauline Baynes', the artist whose drawings had embellished his *Farmer*

Giles of Ham in 1949 and the cover of the Puffin Books *Hobbit* which had then recently appeared (4 October 1961, *Letters*, p. 308). On 11 October, Tolkien sent this idea to Rayner Unwin, of the publishers George Allen & Unwin, noting that the 'Bombadil' poem was 'very pictorial', and that if Pauline Baynes 'could be induced to illustrate it, it might do well' (Tolkien–George Allen & Unwin archive, HarperCollins, hereafter 'A&U archive'; quoted in Scull and Hammond, *The J.R.R. Tolkien Companion and Guide: Chronology* (2006), p. 579).

Unwin agreed, but asked Tolkien to collect other occasional verses, in order to make up a book of a length reasonable for sales. Tolkien had in mind a small volume like *The Tale of Peter Rabbit* by Beatrix Potter; nonetheless, by 15 November, as he wrote to Unwin, he 'made a search, as far as time allowed, and had copies made of any poems that might conceivably see the light or (somewhat tidied up) be presented again. The harvest is not rich, for one thing there is not much that really goes together with Tom Bombadil.' Among the poems gathered up were *Errantry* and *The Man in the Moon Came Down Too Soon*, 'which might go together'. 'About the others', he continued, referring to *Perry-the-Winkle*, *The Sea-Bell*, *The Hoard*, and *The Dragon's Visit*, 'I am altogether doubtful; I do not even know if they have any virtue at all, by themselves or in a series' (*Letters*, p. 309).

Writing on 15 November also to Jane Neave, Tolkien referred to 'raking up' and 'refurbishing' verses published in obscure places, some of which he sent to her, and to the '*Hey Diddle* song and the *Troll Sat Alone*' (*The Man in the Moon Stayed Up Too Late* and *The Stone Troll*), both of which he had included in *The Lord of the Rings* (quoted in Christie's auction catalogue, 2 December 2003, p. 25). A week later, he wrote again to Aunt Jane, having 'enjoyed myself very much digging out these old half-forgotten things and rubbing them up. All the more because there are other and duller things that I ought to have been doing. At any rate they have had you as an audience. Printed publication is, I fear, very unlikely' (22 November, *Letters*, p. 309). With this letter, he enclosed a copy of another poem, *Princess Mee*.

Rayner Unwin sent copies of the verses he had received to Pauline Baynes, and Tolkien himself wrote to her on 23 November. The artist replied to both letters favourably. She found the poems dreamlike, to be felt rather than seen, but Tolkien advised her that 'the things sent to you (except the Sea-bell, the poorest, and not one that I [should] really wish to include, at least not with the others) were conceived as a series of very definite, clear and precise, pictures – fantastical, or nonsensical perhaps, but not dream-like!' (6 December, *Letters*, p. 312). On 8 December, Tolkien wrote to Unwin that Baynes had 'a great talent for producing vivid and believable pictures while touching them with a delightful air of fantasy which is largely imported by her fluid and dexterous line. But I do agree heartily with her feeling [expressed in a letter to him] that all the pieces are very different and I have some misgivings about lumping them together. I am inclined to think that the vaguer, more subjective and least successful piece labelled The Sea-Bell ought to come out in any case' (A&U archive; *Chronology*, p. 582).

Before long, Tolkien saw that the proposed collection had turned into something other than he had planned. It was no longer a small book reprinting a single, existing poem, a burden more for illustrator than author. Now, 'looking out, furbishing up, or re-writing of further items to go with Tom Bombadil and Errantry, took a lot of work. . . .' Also, Tolkien still felt 'very uncertain' about his poems, 'and doubt my own judgment or criticism of what has been really a private past-time' (14 December, A&U archive; *Chronology*, p. 582). At Unwin's invitation, however, he 'raked over' his 'collection of old verses', found more 'that might be made use of with a thorough re-handling', and sent his publisher four of these – *Firiel* (later *The Last Ship*), *Shadow-Bride*, *Knocking at the Door* (later *The Mewlips*), and *The Trees of Kortirion*. *Firiel*, he thought, 'apart from the question of whether it is good or bad in its self', might go with the other poems he had sent thus far. But '*The Trees* is too long and too ambitious, and even if considered good enough would probably upset the boat' (letter to Rayner Unwin, 5 February 1962, A&U archive; *Chronology*, pp. 587–8). Tolkien also now suggested that, if still more poems were required, one or two from *The Lord of the Rings* might be added, such as *Oliphaunt* and *The Man in the Moon Stayed Up Too Late* (Frodo's song at the Prancing Pony).

Though he was under much pressure from other matters, and concerned for his wife's health after a fall, Tolkien gave every moment he could spare to the collection, as he told Rayner Unwin on 12 April 1962. He remained unhappy about the poems, indeed he had 'lost all confidence in these things, and all judgement, and unless Pauline Baynes can be inspired by them, I cannot see them making a "book". I do not see why she should be inspired, though I fervently hope that she will be. Some of the things may be good in their way, and all of them privately amuse me; but elderly hobbits are easily pleased.' And yet, he entered fully into the spirit of the work and gave it a needed context and frame:

The various items – all that I now venture to offer, some with misgiving – do not really 'collect'. The only possible link is the fiction that they come from the Shire from about the period of the *Lord of the Rings*. But that fits some uneasily. I have done a good deal of work, trying to make them fit better: if not much to their good, I hope not to their serious detriment. You may note that I have written a new *Bombadil* poem [*Bombadil Goes Boating*], which I hope is adequate to go with the older one, though for its understanding it requires some knowledge of the *L.R.* At any rate it performs the service of further 'integrating' Tom with the world of the *L.R.* into which he was inserted. . . .

I have placed the 16 items in an order: roughly Bilboish, Samlike ['by' Bilbo Baggins and Sam Gamgee], and Dubious. Some kind of order will be necessary, for the scheme of illustration and decoration. But I am not wedded to this arrangement. I am open to criticisms of it – and of any of the items; and to rejections. Miss Baynes is free to re-arrange things to fit her work, if she wishes.

Some kind of 'foreword' might possibly be required. The enclosed is not intended for that purpose! Though one or two of its points might be made more simply. But I found it easier, and more amusing (for myself) to represent to you in the form of a ridiculous editorial fiction what I have done to the verses, and what their references now are. [A&U archive; *Letters*, pp. 314–15]

Here Tolkien refers to sixteen poems, apparently the final selection as published. By 12 February 1962, he had sent twelve to Allen & Unwin: *The Adventures of Tom Bombadil*, *The Dragon's Visit*, *Errantry*, *Firiel* (*The Last Ship*), *The Hoard*, *Knocking at the Door* (*The Mewlips*), *The Man in the Moon Came Down Too Soon*, *Perry-the-Winkle*, *Princess Mee*, *The Sea-Bell*, *Shadow-Bride*, and *The Trees of Kortirion*. *The Trees of Kortirion*, a revision of a much earlier 'Silmarillion' poem, was later published in *The Book of Lost Tales, Part One* (1983). Christopher Tolkien, the youngest son and literary executor of J.R.R. Tolkien, has speculated that his father also revised another early work, *You & Me and the Cottage of Lost Play*, in the process of 'rubbing up' his old poems.

Rayner Unwin agreed that *The Trees of Kortirion* should be omitted, and *The Dragon's Visit* was deleted as well: this account of a dragon set upon by a fire brigade may have proved too difficult to bring into the world of Hobbits. (First published in the *Oxford Magazine*, *The Dragon's Visit* was reprinted in *The Annotated Hobbit* (1988, 2002), and appeared in revised form in the anthologies *Winter's Tales for Children 1* (1965) and *The Young Magicians* (1969).) To fill out the collection, Tolkien added three poems from *The Lord of the Rings*, *The Man in the Moon Stayed Up Too Late*, *Oliphaunt*, and *The Stone Troll*; his new 'Bombadil' poem, *Bombadil Goes Boating*; *Cat*, which he had written for his granddaughter Joanna in 1956; and a 'bestiary' poem revised from an earlier work, *Fastitocalon*. The final arrangement groups like with like as far as possible. The two 'Bombadil' poems are followed by two 'fairy' poems, two with the Man in the Moon, and two with trolls; then *The Mewlips*, an odd man out, placed near the centre; and finally, three 'bestiary' poems and four with 'atmosphere' and emotion.

Pleased with this selection, and with Tolkien's 'editorial fiction' that the works came from the same 'source' as *The Hobbit* and *The Lord of the Rings* – the 'Red Book of Westmarch' – Rayner Unwin chose to publish the poetry volume for Christmas 1962. Pauline Baynes was now formally engaged to make the illustrations, but could not begin to do so until the middle of June. Her pictures needed careful planning, in concert with Ronald Eames, art editor for Allen & Unwin: some would be in black and white only, while others would have a second (orange) colour added, and for economy, the extra colour would be printed on only one side of each large sheet that made up a gathering. For content, Baynes asked Tolkien for his thoughts, but he gave her a free hand, warning only that his apparently light-hearted verses had a serious undercurrent, and should not be perceived as merely comic.

By the start of August, Baynes delivered the first of her pictures, including art for the binding and dust-jacket, and by 22 August completed six full-page illustrations. Since Allen & Unwin had allowed for only five, Tolkien was asked to decide which one to exclude. 'Pauline rather carries one away at first sight', he wrote to Rayner Unwin; 'but there is an illustrative as well as a pictorial side to take into account' (29 August 1962, A&U archive; *Chronology*, p. 596). Although he admired her large pictures for *Cat* and *The Man in the Moon Came Down Too Soon*, he felt that each had faults; neither, however, in his view was as deserving of omission as Baynes's full-page illustration for *The Hoard*, which Tolkien criticized for its depiction of the young warrior, and of a dragon lying with its head away from, rather than towards, the entrance to its cave. In the event, all six of the larger illustrations were published, and Baynes revised her art for *The Hoard* (opposite) when the *Bombadil* collection was reprinted in *Poems and Stories* (1980).

Tolkien also decided that he was disappointed with Baynes's cover art once he saw it in proof. A wraparound design, it features the mariner from *Errantry* on the upper cover and a sleeping Tom Bombadil on the lower, with a panoply of birds, fish, and other creatures against a backdrop of earth, sea, and sky. 'Alas!' Tolkien wrote to Ronald Eames, 'it is only now . . . that I observe that as an illustration, especially one to fit the general title, the picture should have been reversed: with Bombadil on the front, and the Ship sailing left, westward!' He was unhappy also with the publisher's choice of lettering for the cover, a 'heavy fat-serifed' type, 'at odds with the style of the picture' (12 September 1962, A&U archive; *Chronology*, p. 597). But Allen & Unwin were working to a tight production schedule, and it was too late to effect any change.

The Adventures of Tom Bombadil and Other Verses from the Red Book was published on 22 November 1962. By then, Tolkien had received advance copies, and Rayner

Unwin had noticed that the full-page art for *Cat* was awkwardly placed within the text of *Fastitocalon* and opposite an illustration for the latter – an accident of layout to allow two-colour printing for both pictures. Unwin and Tolkien agreed that, in any reprint, the order of *Cat* and *Fastitocalon* should be reversed and the art adjusted; this was done with the second Allen & Unwin printing in 1962 (and in the American edition from the first printing in 1963), and has been followed in all subsequent editions.

Tolkien wrote to Stanley Unwin, the chairman of George Allen & Unwin, on 28 November that he was 'agreeably surprised' at reviews of the *Bombadil* volume in the *Times Literary Supplement* and *The Listener*. 'I expected remarks far more snooty and patronizing. Also I was rather pleased, since it seemed that the reviewers had both started out not wanting to be amused, but had failed to maintain their Victorian dignity intact' (*Letters*, p. 322). The *Times Literary Supplement* review of 23 November 1962 (attributed to Alfred Duggan) called Tolkien 'a wordsmith, an ingenious versifier, rather than a discoverer of new insights', while Anthony Thwaite in *The Listener* (22 November) contrasted the 'heavy-footed donnish waggery' of Tolkien's preface with the poems, which were 'by turns gay, prattling, melancholy, nonsensical, mysterious. And what is most exciting and attractive about them is their superb technical skill. Professor Tolkien revealed in the verses scattered through *The Hobbit* that he had a talent for songs, riddling rhymes, and a kind of balladry. In *The Adventures of Tom Bombadil* the talent can be seen to be something close to genius.' In response to the latter, Tolkien wondered to Stanley Unwin 'why if a "professor" shows any knowledge of his professional techniques it must be "waggery", but if a writer shows, say, knowledge of law or law-courts it is held interesting and creditable' (28 November, *Letters*, p. 322). It seems likely that Tolkien also saw the review by Christopher Derrick in the Roman Catholic journal *The Tablet* (15 December 1962), which defended the *Bombadil* volume from charges of 'whimsy'. With only a few exceptions, the book received positive reviews.

On 19 December, Tolkien was pleased to tell his son Michael that '"T.B." sold nearly 8,000 copies before publication (caught on the hop they have had to reprint hastily), and that, even on a minute initial royalty, means more than is at all usual for anyone but [popular poet John] Betjeman to make on verse!' (*Letters*, p. 322). On 23 December, he also wrote to Pauline Baynes that the collection was selling uncommonly well (for verse), and attributed its success in large part to her illustrations.

In 1952, Tolkien had recited *The Man in the Moon Stayed Up Too Late*, *Oliphaunt*, and *The Stone Troll* (the latter with variations) into a tape recorder owned by his friend George Sayer: these readings were issued first on a vinyl record in 1975, with other excerpts from *The Lord of the Rings* and *The Hobbit*. In 1967, he made a commercial recording of *The Adventures of Tom Bombadil*, *The Hoard*, *The Man in the Moon Came Down Too Soon*, *The Mewlips*, *Perry-the-Winkle*, and *The Sea-Bell* for the album *Poems and Songs of Middle Earth*, which also featured *Errantry* performed by baritone William Elvin and composer Donald Swann, within Swann's Tolkien song cycle *The Road Goes Ever On*. Tolkien also recorded at this session *Errantry* and *Princess Mee*, but these were issued only in 2001, with Tolkien's other readings from 1967 and his recordings with George Sayer, as part of *The J.R.R. Tolkien Audio Collection*.

Although the preface and poems of *The Adventures of Tom Bombadil and Other Verses from the Red Book* have remained in print since 1962, they have not consistently appeared in a dedicated volume, rather than within a larger collection of shorter works. We are pleased to present them afresh, and to include for comparison earlier printed or manuscript versions (where earlier versions exist). It seems appropriate also to reprint another poem by Tolkien featuring Tom and Goldberry, *Once upon a Time*, first published three years after the *Bombadil* volume appeared, and a possible precursor, *An Evening in Tavrobel*.

Throughout this book, we follow the convention of referring to Tolkien's larger mythology as 'The Silmarillion', in quotation marks, and the edition of its component tales published in 1977 as *The Silmarillion*, italicized. We have assumed, as Tolkien himself did in the preface to the *Bombadil* collection, that the reader has a certain degree of familiarity with (at least) *The Lord of the Rings*.

We are grateful to the Tolkien Estate for permission to reprint or newly publish writings by J.R.R. Tolkien; and for their assistance at many points in the making of this book, we are indebted to Christopher Tolkien, to Cathleen Blackburn of the solicitors Maier Blackburn, to the staff of the Bodleian Libraries, including Colin Harris, Catherine Parker, and Judith Priestman, and to the editors and production staff of HarperCollins, in particular David Brawn, Terence Caven, and Natasha Hughes. We also would like to thank Sr. Joan Breen and Sr. Barbara Jeffery of the Institute of Our Lady of Mercy, Bermondsey, for providing a copy of *The Shadow*

Man from the *Annual* of Our Lady's School, Abingdon, and Stephen Oliver of Our Lady's School for facilitating this contact; and as always, Carl F. Hostetter and Arden R. Smith for helpful advice on Tolkien's invented languages.

Christina Scull & Wayne G. Hammond
January 2014

ABOUT THE ARTIST

Pauline Baynes (1922–2008), born in Hove, East Sussex, spent her early years in India, where her father was a government official, before settling in Surrey. She was a poor student, but had a natural talent for art. She followed her sister Angela to the Farnham School of Art and (informally) to the Slade, but for the most part was self-taught, working mainly in ink and gouache. She was inspired especially by Persian and medieval manuscript decoration, by contemporary artists such as Rex Whistler, and by the natural landscape around her country home.

The Second World War took her to the camouflage development centre at Farnham Castle, where she made models. Another member of staff, Powell Perry, commissioned her to illustrate – in her spare time, and probably without pay – *Mythical Monsters*, *Wild Flower Rhymes* (both 1943), and four other titles in his Perry

Colour Books for children, which were cheaply printed by his family's lithography firm. She considered her first 'proper' illustrations to be those she made for Victoria Stevenson's *Clover Magic*, issued in 1944 by the mainstream publisher Country Life. In that same year, her first magazine illustrations appeared in the monthly *Lilliput*.

Although she had little to show as a professional illustrator, in 1948 Baynes was one of five artists invited by the publisher George Allen & Unwin to submit specimens if she wished to illustrate an 'adult fairytale' then in production. By good luck, she included in her portfolio pseudo-Anglo-Saxon cartoons in a style J.R.R. Tolkien thought exactly right for his mockmedieval *Farmer Giles of Ham*. Later he said of her finished drawings that they reduced his text to a commentary on the art. Her success with *Farmer Giles* (1949) led to even greater fame, when Tolkien's friend C.S. Lewis chose her to illustrate his seven *Chronicles of Narnia* (1950–6). After that, Baynes was usually much in demand.

She was sometimes annoyed that the public tended to know her only as an illustrator for Tolkien and Lewis – her images of Middle-earth and Narnia are as iconic as John Tenniel's for Lewis Carroll's 'Alice' – when in fact she made, in a long career, hundreds of pictures for books and magazines. Some of her most successful art appeared in *A Treasury of French Tales* by Henri Pourrat (1953), Amabel Williams-Ellis's edition of *The Arabian Nights* (1957), *Medieval Tales* by Jennifer Westwood (1967), *A Companion to World Mythology* by Richard Barber (1979), *The Enchanted Horse* by Rosemary Harris (1981), and Baynes's own *Song of the Three Holy Children* (1986). Her illustrations for *A Dictionary of Chivalry* by Grant Uden (1968), which took her years to complete, won the coveted Kate Greenaway medal.

In 1961, at Tolkien's request, Baynes painted a striking cover for the Puffin Books edition of *The Hobbit*. She subsequently had many commissions for Puffin, most famously her 1973 cover for Richard Adams' *Watership Down*. Also in 1961, as explained earlier in this volume, she was asked to illustrate Tolkien's *Tom Bombadil* verses; he thought of her for the book, he said, because she could 'produce wonderful pictures with a touch of "fantasy", but primarily bright and clear visions of things that one might really see'. In 1964, she painted a triptych view of Middle-earth for a boxed set of *The Lord of the Rings*, and in 1967 illustrated Tolkien's *Smith of Wootton Major*. Meanwhile, she and her husband became close friends with Tolkien and his wife, Edith. After Tolkien's death, she made new art for the Tolkien collection *Poems and Stories* (1980) and for his poem *Bilbo's Last Song* (1974, 1990), and drew a map of the Little Kingdom for the fiftieth anniversary edition of *Farmer Giles of Ham* (1999).

The Adventures of Tom Bombadil

and Other Verses from the Red Book

PREFACE

The Red Book contains a large number of verses. A few are included in the narrative of the *Downfall of the Lord of the Rings,* or in the attached stories and chronicles; many more are found on loose leaves, while some are written carelessly in margins and blank spaces. Of the last sort most are nonsense, now often unintelligible even when legible, or half-remembered fragments. From these marginalia are drawn Nos. 4, 11, 13; though a better example of their general character would be the scribble, on the page recording Bilbo's *When winter first begins to bite:*

> *The wind so whirled a weathercock*
> *He could not hold his tail up;*
> *The frost so nipped a throstlecock*
> *He could not snap a snail up.*
> *'My case is hard.' the throstle cried,*

And 'All is vane' the cock replied;
And so they set their wail up.

The present selection is taken from the older pieces, mainly concerned with legends and jests of the Shire at the end of the Third Age, that appear to have been made by Hobbits, especially by Bilbo and his friends, or their immediate descendants. Their authorship is, however, seldom indicated. Those outside the narratives are in various hands, and were probably written down from oral tradition.

In the Red Book it is said that No. 5 was made by Bilbo, and No. 7 by Sam Gamgee. No. 8 is marked SG, and the ascription may be accepted. No. 12 is also marked SG, though at most Sam can only have touched up an older piece of the comic bestiary lore of which Hobbits appear to have been fond. In *The Lord of the Rings* Sam stated that No. 10 was traditional in the Shire.

No. 3 is an example of another kind which seems to have amused Hobbits: a rhyme or story which returns to its own beginning, and so may be recited until the hearers revolt. Several specimens are found in the Red Book, but the others are simple and crude. No. 3 is much the longest and most elaborate. It was evidently made by Bilbo. This is indicated by its obvious relationship to the long poem recited by Bilbo, as his own composition, in the house of Elrond. In origin a 'nonsense rhyme', it is in the Rivendell version found transformed and applied, somewhat incongruously, to the High-elvish and Númenórean legends of Eärendil. Probably because Bilbo invented its metrical devices and was proud of them. They do not appear in other pieces in the Red Book. The older form, here given, must belong to the early days after Bilbo's return from his journey. Though the influence of Elvish traditions is seen, they are not seriously treated, and the names used (*Derrilyn, Thellamie, Belmarie, Aerie*) are mere inventions in the Elvish style, and are not in fact Elvish at all.

The influence of the events at the end of the Third Age, and the widening of the horizons of the Shire by contact with Rivendell and Gondor, is to be seen in other pieces. No. 6, though here placed next to Bilbo's Man-in-the-Moon rhyme, and the last item, No. 16, must be derived ultimately from Gondor. They are evidently based on the traditions of Men, living in shorelands and familiar with rivers running into the Sea. No. 6 actually mentions *Belfalas* (the windy bay of Bel), and the Seaward Tower, *Tirith Aear*, of Dol Amroth. No. 16 mentions the Seven Rivers[1] that flowed into the Sea in the South

---

1   *Lefnui, Morthond-Kiril-Ringló, Gilrain-Serni,* and *Anduin.*

Kingdom, and uses the Gondorian name, of High-elvish form, *Firiel*, mortal woman.[1] In the Langstrand and Dol Amroth there were many traditions of the ancient Elvish dwellings, and of the haven at the mouth of the Morthond from which 'westward ships' had sailed as far back as the fall of Eregion in the Second Age. These two pieces, therefore, are only re-handlings of Southern matter, though this may have reached Bilbo by way of Rivendell. No. 14 also depends on the lore of Rivendell, Elvish and Númenórean, concerning the heroic days at the end of the First Age; it seems to contain echoes of the Númenorean tale of Túrin and Mîm the Dwarf.

Nos. 1 and 2 evidently come from the Buckland. They show more knowledge of that country, and of the Dingle, the wooded valley of the Withywindle,[2] than any Hobbits west of the Marish were likely to possess.

---

[1] The name was borne by a princess of Gondor, through whom Aragorn claimed descent from the Southern line. It was also the name of a daughter of Elanor, daughter of Sam, but her name, if connected with the rhyme, must be derived from it; it could not have arisen in Westmarch.

[2] *Grindwall* was a small hythe on the north bank of the Withywindle; it was outside the Hay, and so was well watched and protected by a grind or fence extended into the water. *Breredon* (Briar Hill) was a little village on rising ground behind the hythe, in the narrow tongue between the end of the High Hay and the Brandywine. At the *Mithe*, the outflow of the Shire-bourn, was a landing-stage, from which a lane ran to Deephallow and so on to the Causeway road that went through Rushey and Stock.

They also show that the Bucklanders knew Bombadil,[1] though, no doubt, they had as little understanding of his powers as the Shirefolk had of Gandalf's: both were regarded as benevolent persons, mysterious maybe and unpredictable but nonetheless comic. No. 1 is the earlier piece, and is made up of various hobbit-versions of legends concerning Bombadil. No. 2 uses similar traditions, though Tom's raillery is here turned in jest upon his friends, who treat it with amusement (tinged with fear); but it was probably composed much later and after the visit of Frodo and his companions to the house of Bombadil.

The verses, of hobbit origin, here presented have generally two features in common. They are fond of strange words, and of rhyming and metrical tricks – in their simplicity Hobbits evidently regarded such things as virtues or graces, though they were, no doubt, mere imitations of Elvish practices. They are also, at least on the surface, lighthearted or frivolous, though sometimes one may uneasily suspect that more is meant than meets the ear. No. 15, certainly of hobbit origin, is an exception. It is the latest piece and belongs to the Fourth Age; but it is included here, because a hand has

---

[1] Indeed they probably gave him this name (it is Bucklandish in form) to add to his many older ones.

scrawled at its head *Frodos Dreme*. That is remarkable, and though the piece is most unlikely to have been written by Frodo himself, the title shows that it was associated with the dark and despairing dreams which visited him in March and October during his last three years. But there were certainly other traditions, concerning Hobbits that were taken by the 'wandering-madness', and if they ever returned, were afterwards queer and uncommunicable. The thought of the Sea was ever-present in the background of hobbit imagination; but fear of it and distrust of all Elvish lore, was the prevailing mood in the Shire at the end of the Third Age, and that mood was certainly not entirely dispelled by the events and changes with which that Age ended.

1

THE ADVENTURES
OF TOM BOMBADIL

Old Tom Bombadil was a merry fellow;
bright blue his jacket was and his boots were yellow,
green were his girdle and his breeches all of leather;
he wore in his tall hat a swan-wing feather.
He lived up under Hill, where the Withywindle
ran from a grassy well down into the dingle.

Old Tom in summertime walked about the meadows
gathering the buttercups, running after shadows,
tickling the bumblebees that buzzed among the
     flowers,
sitting by the waterside for hours upon hours.

There his beard dangled long down into the water:
up came Goldberry, the River-woman's daughter;
pulled Tom's hanging hair. In he went a-wallowing
under the water-lilies, bubbling and a-swallowing.

'Hey, Tom Bombadil! Whither are you going?'
said fair Goldberry. 'Bubbles you are blowing,
frightening the finny fish and the brown water-rat,
startling the dabchicks, and drowning your
      feather-hat!'

'You bring it back again, there's a pretty maiden!'
said Tom Bombadil. 'I do not care for wading.
Go down! Sleep again where the pools are shady
far below willow-roots, little water-lady!'

Back to her mother's house in the deepest hollow
swam young Goldberry. But Tom, he would not
      follow;
on knotted willow-roots he sat in sunny weather,
drying his yellow boots and his draggled feather.

Up woke Willow-man, began upon his singing,
sang Tom fast asleep under branches swinging;
in a crack caught him tight: snick! it closed together,
trapped Tom Bombadil, coat and hat and feather.

'Ha, Tom Bombadil! What be you a-thinking,
peeping inside my tree, watching me a-drinking

deep in my wooden house, tickling me with feather,
dripping wet down my face like a rainy weather?'

'You let me out again, Old Man Willow!
I am stiff lying here; they're no sort of pillow,
your hard crooked roots. Drink your river-water!
Go back to sleep again like the River-daughter!'

Willow-man let him loose when he heard him
        speaking;
locked fast his wooden house, muttering and creaking,
whispering inside the tree. Out from willow-dingle
Tom went walking on up the Withywindle.
Under the forest-eaves he sat a while a-listening:
on the boughs piping birds were chirruping and
        whistling.
Butterflies about his head went quivering and winking,
until grey clouds came up, as the sun was sinking.

Then Tom hurried on. Rain began to shiver,
round rings spattering in the running river;
a wind blew, shaken leaves chilly drops were dripping;
into a sheltering hole Old Tom went skipping.

Out came Badger-brock with his snowy forehead
and his dark blinking eyes. In the hill he quarried
with his wife and many sons. By the coat they caught
    him,
pulled him inside their earth, down their tunnels
    brought him.

Inside their secret house, there they sat a-mumbling:
'Ho, Tom Bombadil! Where have you come tumbling,
bursting in the front-door? Badger-folk have caught you.
You'll never find it out, the way that we have brought
    you!'

'Now, old Badger-brock, do you hear me talking?
You show me out at once! I must be a-walking.
Show me to your backdoor under briar-roses;
then clean grimy paws, wipe your earthy noses!
Go back to sleep again on your straw pillow,
like fair Goldberry and Old Man Willow!'

Then all the Badger-folk said: 'We beg your pardon!'
They showed Tom out again to their thorny garden,
went back and hid themselves, a-shivering and
    a-shaking,
blocked up all their doors, earth together raking.

Rain had passed. The sky was clear, and in the
    summer-gloaming
Old Tom Bombadil laughed as he came homing,
unlocked his door again, and opened up a shutter.
In the kitchen round the lamp moths began to flutter;
Tom through the window saw waking stars come
    winking,
and the new slender moon early westward sinking.

Dark came under Hill. Tom, he lit a candle;
upstairs creaking went, turned the door-handle.
'Hoo, Tom Bombadil! Look what night has brought
    you!
I'm here behind the door. Now at last I've caught you!
You'd forgotten Barrow-wight dwelling in the old
    mound
up there on hill-top with the ring of stones round.
He's got loose again. Under earth he'll take you.
Poor Tom Bombadil, pale and cold he'll make you!'

'Go out! Shut the door, and never come back after!
Take away gleaming eyes, take your hollow laughter!
Go back to grassy mound, on your stony pillow
lay down your bony head, like Old Man Willow,

like young Goldberry, and Badger-folk in burrow!
Go back to buried gold and forgotten sorrow!'

Out fled Barrow-wight through the window leaping,
through the yard, over wall like a shadow sweeping,
up hill wailing went back to leaning stone-rings,
back under lonely mound, rattling his bone-rings.

Old Tom Bombadil lay upon his pillow
sweeter than Goldberry, quieter than the Willow,
snugger than the Badger-folk or the Barrow-dwellers;
slept like a humming-top, snored like a bellows.

He woke in morning-light, whistled like a starling,
sang, 'Come, derry-dol, merry-dol, my darling!'
He clapped on his battered hat, boots, and coat and
        feather;
opened the window wide to the sunny weather.

Wise old Bombadil, he was a wary fellow;
bright blue his jacket was, and his boots were yellow.
None ever caught old Tom in upland or in dingle,
walking the forest-paths, or by the Withywindle,
or out on the lily-pools in boat upon the water.

But one day Tom, he went and caught the
    River-daughter,
in green gown, flowing hair, sitting in the rushes,
singing old water-songs to birds upon the bushes.

He caught her, held her fast! Water-rats went
    scuttering
reeds hissed, herons cried, and her heart was fluttering.
Said Tom Bombadil: 'Here's my pretty maiden!
You shall come home with me! The table is all laden:
yellow cream, honeycomb, white bread and butter;
roses at the window-sill and peeping round the
    shutter.
You shall come under Hill! Never mind your mother
in her deep weedy pool: there you'll find no lover!'

Old Tom Bombadil had a merry wedding,
crowned all with buttercups, hat and feather shedding;
his bride with forgetmenots and flag-lilies for garland
was robed all in silver-green. He sang like a starling,
hummed like a honey-bee, lilted to the fiddle,
clasping his river-maid round her slender middle.

Lamps gleamed within his house, and white was the
    bedding;

in the bright honey-moon Badger-folk came treading,
danced down under Hill, and Old Man Willow
tapped, tapped at window-pane, as they slept on the
     pillow,
on the bank in the reeds River-woman sighing
heard old Barrow-wight in his mound crying.

Old Tom Bombadil heeded not the voices,
taps, knocks, dancing feet, all the nightly noises;
slept till the sun arose, then sang like a starling:
'Hey! Come derry-dol, merry-dol, my darling!'
sitting on the door-step chopping sticks of willow,
while fair Goldberry combed her tresses yellow.

2

BOMBADIL GOES BOATING

The old year was turning brown; the West Wind was
    calling;
Tom caught a beechen leaf in the Forest falling.
'I've caught a happy day blown me by the breezes!
Why wait till morrow-year? I'll take it when me
    pleases.
This day I'll mend my boat and journey as it chances
west down the withy-stream, following my fancies!'

Little Bird sat on twig. 'Whillo, Tom! I heed you.
I've a guess, I've a guess where your fancies lead you.
Shall I go, shall I go, bring him word to meet you?'

'No names, you tell-tale, or I'll skin and eat you,
babbling in every ear things that don't concern you!
If you tell Willow-man where I've gone, I'll burn you,
roast you on a willow-spit. That'll end your prying!'

Willow-wren cocked her tail, piped as she went flying:
'Catch me first, catch me first! No names are needed.
I'll perch on his hither ear: the message will be heeded.
"Down by Mithe," I'll say, "just as sun is sinking."
Hurry up, hurry up! That's the time for drinking!'

Tom laughed to himself: 'Maybe then I'll go there.
I might go by other ways, but today I'll row there.'
He shaved oars, patched his boat; from hidden creek
    he hauled her
through reed and sallow-brake, under leaning alder,
then down the river went, singing: 'Silly-sallow,
Flow withy-willow-stream over deep and shallow!'

'Whee! Tom Bombadil! Whither be you going,
bobbing in a cockle-boat, down the river rowing?'

'Maybe to Brandywine along the Withywindle;
maybe friends of mind fire for me will kindle
down by the Hays-end. Little folk I know there,
kind at the day's end. Now and then I go there.'

'Take word to my kin, bring me back their tidings!
Tell me of diving pools and the fishes' hidings!'

'Nay then,' said Bombadil, 'I am only rowing
just to smell the water like, not on errands going.'

'Tee hee! Cocky Tom! Mind your tub don't founder!
Look out for willow-snags! I'd laugh to see you
        flounder.'

'Talk less, Fisher Blue! Keep your kindly wishes!
Fly off and preen yourself with the bones of fishes!
Gay lord on your bough, at home a dirty varlet
living in a sloven house, though your breast be scarlet.
I've heard of fisher-birds beak in air a-dangling
to show how the wind is set: that's an end of angling!'

The King's fisher shut his beak, winked his eye, as
        singing
Tom passed under bough. Flash! then he went
        winging;
dropped down jewel-blue a feather, and Tom caught it
gleaming in a sun-ray: a pretty gift he thought it.
He stuck it in his tall hat, the old feather casting:
'Blue now for Tom,' he said, 'a merry hue and lasting!'

Rings swirled round his boat, he saw the bubbles
    quiver.
Tom slapped his oar, smack! at a shadow in the river.
'Hoosh! Tom Bombadil! 'Tis long since last I met you.
Turned water-boatman, eh? What if I upset you?'

'What? Why, Whisker-lad, I'd ride you down the river.
My fingers on your back would set your hide a-shiver.'

'Pish, Tom Bombadil! I'll go and tell my mother;
"Call all our kin to come, father, sister, brother!
Tom's gone mad as a coot with wooden legs: he's
    paddling
down Withywindle stream, an old tub a-straddling!"'

'I'll give your otter-fell to Barrow-wights. They'll taw
    you!
Then smother you in gold-rings! Your mother if she
    saw you,
she'd never know her son, unless 'twas by a whisker.
Nay, don't tease old Tom, until you be far brisker!'

'Whoosh!' said otter-lad, river-water spraying
over Tom's hat and all; set the boat a-swaying,

dived down under it, and by the bank lay peering,
till Tom's merry song faded out of hearing.

Old Swan of Elvet-isle sailed past him proudly,
gave Tom a black look, snorted at him loudly.
Tom laughed: 'You old cob, do you miss your feather?
Give me a new one then! The old was worn by
    weather.
Could you speak a fair word, I would love you dearer:
long neck and dumb throat, but still a haughty sneerer!
If one day the King returns, in upping he may take you,
brand your yellow bill, and less lordly make you!'
Old Swan huffed his wings, hissed, and paddled
    faster;
in his wake bobbing on Tom went rowing after.

Tom came to Withy-weir. Down the river rushing
foamed into Windle-reach, a-bubbling and a-splashing;
bore Tom over stone spinning like a windfall,
bobbing like a bottle-cork, to the hythe at Grindwall.

'Hoy! Here's Woodman Tom with his billy-beard on!'
laughed all the little folk of Hays-end and Breredon.
'Ware, Tom! We'll shoot you dead with our bows and
    arrows!

We don't let Forest-folk nor bogies from the Barrows
cross over Brandywine by cockle-boat nor ferry.'
'Fie, little fatbellies! Don't ye make so merry!
I've seen hobbit-folk digging holes to hide 'em,
frightened if a horny goat or a badger eyed 'em,
afeared of the moony-beams, their old shadows
    shunning.
I'll call the orks on you: that'll send you running!'

'You may call, Woodman Tom. And you can talk your
    beard off.
Three arrows in your hat! You we're not afeared of!
Where would you go to now? If for beer you're making,
the barrels aint deep enough in Breredon for your
    slaking!'

'Away over Brandywine by Shirebourn I'd be going,
but too swift for cockle-boat the river now is flowing.
I'd bless little folk that took me in their wherry,
wish them evenings fair and many mornings merry.'

Red flowed the Brandywine; with flame the river
    kindled,
as sun sank beyond the Shire, and then to grey it
    dwindled.

Mithe Steps empty stood. None was there to greet him.
Silent the Causeway lay. Said Tom: 'A merry meeting!'

Tom stumped along the road, as the light was failing.
Rushey lamps gleamed ahead. He heard a voice him
    hailing.
'Whoa there!' Ponies stopped, wheels halted sliding.
Tom went plodding past, never looked beside him.

'Ho there! beggarman tramping in the Marish!
What's your business here? Hat all stuck with arrows!
Someone's warned you off, caught you at your
    sneaking?
Come here! Tell me now what it is you're seeking!
Shire-ale, I'll be bound, though you've not a penny.
I'll bid them lock their doors, and then you won't get
    any!'

'Well, well, Muddy-feet! From one that's late for
    meeting
away back by the Mithe that's a surly greeting!
You old farmer fat that cannot walk for wheezing,
cart-drawn like a sack, ought to be more pleasing.
Penny-wise tub-on-legs! A beggar can't be chooser,
or else I'd bid you go, and you would be the loser.

Come, Maggot! Help me up! A tankard now you
    owe me.
Even in cockshut light an old friend should know me!'

Laughing they drove away, in Rushey never halting,
though the inn open stood and they could smell the
    malting.
They turned down Maggot's Lane, rattling and
    bumping,
Tom in the farmer's cart dancing round and jumping.
Stars shone on Bamfurlong, and Maggot's house was
    lighted;
fire in the kitchen burned to welcome the benighted.

Maggot's sons bowed at door, his daughters did their
    curtsy,
his wife brought tankards out for those that might be
    thirsty.
Songs they had and merry tales, the supping and the
    dancing;
Goodman Maggot there for all his belt was prancing,
Tom did a hornpipe when he was not quaffing,
daughters did the Springle-ring, goodwife did the
    laughing.

When others went to bed in hay, fern, or feather,
close in the inglenook they laid their heads together,
old Tom and Muddy-feet, swapping all the tidings
from Barrow-downs to Tower Hills: of walkings and of
     ridings;
of wheat-ear and barley-corn, of sowing and of reaping;
queer tales from Bree, and talk at smithy, mill, and
     cheaping;
rumours in whispering trees, south-wind in the larches,
tall Watchers by the Ford, Shadows on the marches.

Old Maggot slept at last in chair beside the embers.
Ere dawn Tom was gone: as dreams one half
     remembers,
some merry, some sad, and some of hidden warning.
None heard the door unlocked; a shower of rain at
     morning
his footprints washed away, at Mithe he left no traces,
at Hays-end they heard no song nor sound of heavy
     paces.

Three days his boat lay by the hythe at Grindwall,
and then one morn was gone back up Withywindle.
Otter-folk, hobbits said, came by night and loosed her,
dragged her over weir, and up stream they pushed her.

Out from Elvet-isle Old Swan came sailing,
in beak took her painter up in the water trailing,
drew her proudly on; otters swam beside her
round old Willow-man's crooked roots to guide her;
the King's fisher perched on bow, on thwart the wren
    was singing,
merrily the cockle-boat homeward they were bringing.
To Tom's creek they came at last. Otter-lad said:
    'Whish now!
What's a coot without his legs, or a finless fish now?'
O! silly-sallow-willow-stream! The oars they'd left
    behind them!
Long they lay at Grindwall hythe for Tom to come
    and find them.

3
ERRANTRY

There was a merry passenger,
a messenger, a mariner:
he built a gilded gondola
to wander in, and had in her
a load of yellow oranges
and porridge for his provender;
he perfumed her with marjoram
and cardamom and lavender.

He called the winds of argosies
with cargoes in to carry him
across the rivers seventeen
that lay between to tarry him.
He landed all in loneliness
where stonily the pebbles on
the running river Derrilyn
goes merrily for ever on.

He journeyed then through meadow-lands
to Shadow-land that dreary lay,
and under hill and over hill
went roving still a weary way.

He sat and sang a melody,
his errantry a-tarrying;
he begged a pretty butterfly
that fluttered by to marry him.
She scorned him and she scoffed at him,
she laughed at him unpitying;
so long he studied wizardry
and sigaldry and smithying.

He wove a tissue airy-thin
to snare her in; to follow her
he made him beetle-leather wing
and feather wing of swallow-hair.
He caught her in bewilderment
with filament of spider-thread;
he made her soft pavilions
of lilies, and a bridal bed
of flowers and of thistle-down
to nestle down and rest her in;

and silken webs of filmy white
and silver light he dressed her in.

He threaded gems in necklaces,
but recklessly she squandered them
and fell to bitter quarrelling;
then sorrowing he wandered on,
and there he left her withering,
as shivering he fled away;
with windy weather following
on swallow-wing he sped away.

He passed the archipelagoes
where yellow grows the marigold,
where countless silver fountains are,
and mountains arc of fairy-gold.
He took to war and foraying,
a-harrying beyond the sea,
and roaming over Belmarie
and Thellamie and Fantasie.

He made a shield and morion
of coral and of ivory,
a sword he made of emerald,
and terrible his rivalry

with elven-knights of Aerie
and Faerie, with paladins
that golden-haired and shining-eyed
came riding by and challenged him.

Of crystal was his habergeon,
his scabbard of chalcedony;
with silver tipped at plenilune
his spear was hewn of ebony.
His javelins were of malachite

and stalactite — he brandished them,
and went and fought the dragon-flies
of Paradise, and vanquished them.

He battled with the Dumbledors,
the Hummerhorns, and Honeybees,
and won the Golden Honeycomb;
and running home on sunny seas
in ship of leaves and gossamer
with blossom for a canopy,
he sat and sang, and furbished up
and burnished up his panoply.

He tarried for a little while
in little isles that lonely lay,

and found there naught but blowing grass;
and so at last the only way
he took, and turned, and coming home
with honeycomb, to memory
his message came, and errand too!
In derring-do and glamoury
he had forgot them, journeying
and tourneying, a wanderer.
So now he must depart again
and start again his gondola,
for ever still a messenger,
a passenger, a tarrier,
a-roving as a feather does,
a weather-driven mariner.

4

PRINCESS MEE

Little Princess Mee
Lovely was she
As in elven-song is told:
    She had pearls in hair
    All threaded fair;
Of gossamer shot with gold
    Was her kerchief made,
    And a silver braid
Of stars about her throat.
    Of moth-web light
    All moonlit-white
She wore a woven coat,
    And round her kirtle
    Was bound a girdle
Sewn with diamond dew.

    She walked by day
    Under mantle grey

And hood of clouded blue;
    But she went by night
    All glittering bright
Under the starlit sky,
    And her slippers frail
    Of fishes' mail
Flashed as she went by
    To her dancing-pool,
    And on mirror cool
Of windless water played.
    As a mist of light
    In whirling flight
A glint like glass she made
    Wherever her feet
    Of silver fleet
Flicked the dancing-floor.

    She looked on high
    To the roofless sky,
And she looked to the shadowy shore;
    Then round she went,
    And her eyes she bent
And saw beneath her go
    A Princess Shee

As fair as Mee:
They were dancing toe to toe!

Shee was as light
As Mee, and as bright;
But Shee was, strange to tell,
Hanging down
With starry crown
Into a bottomless well!
Her gleaming eyes
In great surprise
Looked up to the eyes of Mee:
A marvellous thing,
Head-down to swing
Above a starry sea!

Only their feet
Could ever meet;
For where the ways might lie
To find a land
Where they do not stand
But hang down in the sky
No one could tell
Nor learn in spell

In all the elven-lore.
So still on her own
An elf alone
Dancing as before
With pearls in hair
And kirtle fair
And slippers frail
Of fishes' mail went Mee:
Of fishes' mail
And slippers frail
And kirtle fair
With pearls in hair went Shee!

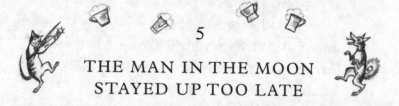

5

THE MAN IN THE MOON
STAYED UP TOO LATE

There is an inn, a merry old inn
   beneath an old grey hill,
And there they brew a beer so brown
That the Man in the Moon himself came down
   one night to drink his fill.

The ostler has a tipsy cat
   that plays a five-stringed fiddle;
And up and down he runs his bow,
Now squeaking high, now purring low,
   now sawing in the middle.

The landlord keeps a little dog
   that is mighty fond of jokes;
When there's good cheer among the guests,
He cocks an ear at all the jests
   and laughs until he chokes.

They also keep a hornéd cow
   as proud as any queen;
But music turns her head like ale,
And makes her wave her tufted tail
   and dance upon the green.

And O! the row of silver dishes
   and the store of silver spoons!
For Sunday there's a special pair,
And these they polish up with care
   on Saturday afternoons.

The Man in the Moon was drinking deep,
   and the cat began to wail;
A dish and a spoon on the table danced,
The cow in the garden madly pranced,
   and the little dog chased his tail.

The Man in the Moon took another mug,
   and then rolled beneath his chair;
And there he dozed and dreamed of ale,
Till in the sky the stars were pale,
   and dawn was in the air.

The ostler said to his tipsy cat:
   'The white horses of the Moon,
They neigh and champ their silver bits;
But their master's been and drowned his wits,
   and the Sun'll be rising soon!'

So the cat on his fiddle played hey-diddle-diddle,
   a jig that would wake the dead:
He squeaked and sawed and quickened the tune,
While the landlord shook the Man in the Moon:
   'It's after three!' he said.

They rolled the Man slowly up the hill
   and bundled him into the Moon,
While his horses galloped up in rear,
And the cow came capering like a deer,
   and a dish ran up with a spoon.

Now quicker the fiddle went deedle-dum-diddle;
   the dog began to roar,
The cow and the horses stood on their heads;
The guests all bounded from their beds
   and danced upon the floor.

With a ping and a pong the fiddle-strings broke!
   the cow jumped over the Moon,
And the little dog laughed to see such fun,
And the Saturday dish went off at a run
   with the silver Sunday spoon.

The round Moon rolled behind the hill,
   as the Sun raised up her head.
She hardly believed her fiery eyes;
For though it was day, to her surprise
   they all went back to bed!

6

THE MAN IN THE MOON
CAME DOWN TOO SOON

The Man in the Moon had silver shoon,
    and his beard was of silver thread;
With opals crowned and pearls all bound
    about his girdlestead,
In his mantle grey he walked one day
    across a shining floor,
And with crystal key in secrecy
    he opened an ivory door.

On a filigree stair of glimmering hair
    then lightly down he went,
And merry was he at last to be free
    on a mad adventure bent.
In diamonds white he had lost delight;
    he was tired of his minaret
Of tall moonstone that towered alone
    on a lunar mountain set.

He would dare any peril for ruby and beryl
  to broider his pale attire,
For new diadems of lustrous gems,
  emerald and sapphire.
He was lonely too with nothing to do
  but stare at the world of gold
And heark to the hum that would distantly come
  as gaily round it rolled.

At plenilune in his argent moon
  in his heart he longed for Fire:
Not the limpid lights of wan selenites;
  for red was his desire,
For crimson and rose and ember-glows,
  for flame with burning tongue,
For the scarlet skies in a swift sunrise
  when a stormy day is young.

He'd have seas of blues, and the living hues
  of forest green and fen;
And he yearned for the mirth of the populous earth
  and the sanguine blood of men.
He coveted song, and laughter long,
  and viands hot, and wine,

Eating pearly cakes of light snowflakes
    and drinking thin moonshine.

He twinkled his feet, as he thought of the meat,
    of pepper, and punch galore;
And he tripped unaware on his slanting stair,
    and like a meteor,
A star in flight, ere Yule one night
    flickering down he fell
From his laddery path to a foaming bath
    in the windy Bay of Bel.

He began to think, lest he melt and sink,
    what in the moon to do,
When a fisherman's boat found him far afloat
    to the amazement of the crew,
Caught in their net all shimmering wet
    in a phosphorescent sheen
Of bluey whites and opal lights
    and delicate liquid green.

Against his wish with the morning fish
    they packed him back to land:
'You had best get a bed in an inn,' they said;
    'the town is near at hand.'

Only the knell of one slow bell
 high in the Seaward Tower
Announced the news of his moonsick cruise
 at that unseemly hour.

Not a hearth was laid, not a breakfast made,
 and dawn was cold and damp.
There were ashes for fire, and for grass the mire,
 for the sun a smoking lamp
In a dim back-street. Not a man did he meet,
 no voice was raised in song;
There were snores instead, for all folk were abed
 and still would slumber long.

He knocked as he passed on doors locked fast,
 and called and cried in vain,
Till he came to an inn that had light within,
 and he tapped at a window-pane.
A drowsy cook gave a surly look,
 and 'What do you want?' said he.
'I want fire and gold and songs of old
 and red wine flowing free!'

'You won't get them here,' said the cook with a leer,
 'but you may come inside.

Silver I lack and silk to my back —
    maybe I'll let you bide.'
A silver gift the latch to lift,
    a pearl to pass the door;
For a seat by the cook in the ingle-nook
    it cost him twenty more.

For hunger or drouth naught passed his mouth
    till he gave both crown and cloak;
And all that he got, in an earthen pot
    broken and black with smoke,
Was porridge cold and two days old
    to eat with a wooden spoon.
For puddings of Yule with plums, poor fool,
    he arrived so much too soon:
An unwary guest on a lunatic quest
    from the Mountains of the Moon.

7

THE STONE TROLL

Troll sat alone on his seat of stone,
And munched and mumbled a bare old bone;
  For many a year he had gnawed it near,
    For meat was hard to come by.
      Done by! Gum by!
  In a cave in the hills he dwelt alone,
    And meat was hard to come by.

Up came Tom with his big boots on.
Said he to Troll: 'Pray, what is yon?
  For it looks like the shin o' my nuncle Tim,
    As should be a-lyin' in graveyard.
      Caveyard! Paveyard!
  This many a year has Tim been gone,
    And I thought he were lyin' in graveyard.'

'My lad,' said Troll, 'this bone I stole.
But what be bones that lie in a hole?

Thy nuncle was dead as a lump o' lead,
　　Afore I found his shinbone.
　　　　Tinbone! Thinbone!
He can spare a share for a poor old troll;
　　For he don't need his shinbone.'

Said Tom: 'I don't see why the likes o' thee
Without axin' leave should go makin' free
　　With the shank or the shin o' my father's kin;
　　　　So hand the old bone over!
　　　　　Rover! Trover!
Though dead he be, it belongs to he;
　　So hand the old bone over!'

'For a couple o' pins,' says Troll, and grins,
'I'll eat thee too, and gnaw thy shins.
　　A bit o' fresh meat will go down sweet!
　　　　I'll try my teeth on thee now.
　　　　　Hee now! See now!
I'm tired o' gnawing old bones and skins;
　　I've a mind to dine on thee now.'

But just as he thought his dinner was caught,
He found his hands had hold of naught.
　　Before he could mind, Tom slipped behind

And gave him the boot to larn him.
    Warn him! Darn him!
A bump o' the boot on the seat, Tom thought,
    Would be the way to larn him.

But harder than stone is the flesh and bone
Of a troll that sits in the hills alone.
    As well set your boot to the mountain's root,
        For the seat of a troll don't feel it.
            Peel it! Heal it!
    Old Troll laughed, when he heard Tom groan,
        And he knew his toes could feel it.

Tom's leg is game, since home he came,
And his bootless foot is lasting lame;
    But Troll don't care, and he's still there
        With the bone he boned from its owner.
            Doner! Boner!
    Troll's old seat is still the same,
        And the bone he boned from its owner!

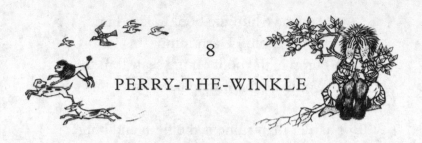

8

PERRY-THE-WINKLE

The Lonely Troll he sat on a stone
　　and sang a mournful lay:
'O why, O why must I live on my own
　　in the hills of Faraway?
My folk are gone beyond recall
　　and take no thought of me;
alone I'm left, the last of all
　　from Weathertop to the Sea.'

'I steal no gold, I drink no beer,
　　I eat no kind of meat;
but People slam their doors in fear,
　　whenever they hear my feet.
O how I wish that they were neat,
　　and my hands were not so rough!
Yet my heart is soft, my smile is sweet,
　　and my cooking good enough.'

'Come, come!' he thought, 'this will not do!
    I must go and find a friend;
a-walking soft I'll wander through
    the Shire from end to end.'
Down he went, and he walked all night
    with his feet in boots of fur;
to Delving he came in the morning light,
    when folk were just astir.

He looked around, and who did he meet
    but old Mrs. Bunce and all
with umbrella and basket walking the street;
    and he smiled and stopped to call:
'Good morning, ma'am! Good day to you!
    I hope I find you well?'
But she dropped umbrella and basket too,
    and yelled a frightful yell.

Old Pott the Mayor was strolling near;
    when he heard that awful sound,
he turned all purple and pink with fear,
    and dived down underground.
The Lonely Troll was hurt and sad:
    'Don't go!' he gently said,

but old Mrs. Bunce ran home like mad
    and hid beneath her bed.

The Troll went on to the market-place
    and peeped above the stalls;
the sheep went wild when they saw his face,
    and the geese flew over the walls.
Old Farmer Hogg he spilled his ale,
    Bill Butcher threw a knife,
and Grip his dog, he turned his tail
    and ran to save his life.

The old Troll sadly sat and wept
    outside the Lockholes gate,
and Perry-the-Winkle up he crept
    and patted him on the pate.
'O why do you weep, you great big lump?
    You're better outside than in!'
He gave the Troll a friendly thump,
    and laughed to see him grin.

'O Perry-the-Winkle boy,' he cried,
    'come, you're the lad for me!
Now if you're willing to take a ride,

I'll carry you home to tea.'
He jumped on his back and held on tight,
    and 'Off you go!' said he;
and the Winkle had a feast that night,
    and sat on the old Troll's knee.

There were pikelets, there was buttered toast,
    and jam, and cream, and cake,
and the Winkle strove to eat the most,
    though his buttons all should break.
The kettle sang, the fire was hot,
    the pot was large and brown,
and the Winkle tried to drink the lot,
    in tea though he should drown.

When full and tight were coat and skin,
    they rested without speech,
till the old Troll said: 'I'll now begin
    the baker's art to teach,
the making of beautiful cramsome bread,
    of bannocks light and brown;
and then you can sleep on a heather-bed
    with pillows of owlet's down.'

'Young Winkle, where've you been?' they said.
    'I've been to a fulsome tea,
and I feel so fat, for I have fed
    on cramsome bread,' said he.
'But where, my lad, in the Shire was that?
    Or out in Bree?' said they.
But Winkle he up and answered flat:
    'I aint a-going to say.'

'But I know where,' said Peeping Jack,
    'I watched him ride away:
he went upon the old Troll's back
    to the hills of Faraway.'
Then all the People went with a will,
    by pony, cart, or moke,
until they came to a house in a hill
    and saw a chimney smoke.

They hammered upon the old Troll's door.
    'A beautiful cramsome cake
O bake for us, please, or two, or more;
    O bake!' they cried, 'O bake!'
'Go home, go home!' the old Troll said.
    'I never invited you.

Only on Thursdays I bake my bread,
   and only for a few.'

'Go home! Go home! There's some mistake.
   My house is far too small;
and I've no pikelets, cream, or cake:
   the Winkle has eaten all!
You Jack, and Hogg, old Bunce and Pott
   I wish no more to see.
Be off! Be off now all the lot!
   The Winkle's the boy for me!'

Now Perry-the-Winkle grew so fat
   through eating of cramsome bread,
his weskit bust, and never a hat
   would sit upon his head;
for Every Thursday he went to tea,
   and sat on the kitchen floor,
and smaller the old Troll seemed to be,
   as he grew more and more.

The Winkle a Baker great became,
   as still is said in song;
from the Sea to Bree there went the fame

of his bread both short and long.
But it weren't so good as the cramsome bread;
    no butter so rich and free,
as Every Thursday the old Troll spread
    for Perry-the-Winkle's tea.

9

THE MEWLIPS

The shadows where the Mewlips dwell
    Are dark and wet as ink,
And slow and softly rings their bell,
    As in the slime you sink.

You sink into the slime, who dare
    To knock upon their door,
While down the grinning gargoyles stare
    And noisome waters pour.

Beside the rotting river-strand
    The drooping willows weep,
And gloomily the gorcrows stand
    Croaking in their sleep.

Over the Merlock Mountains a long and weary way,
   In a mouldy valley where the trees are grey,
By a dark pool's borders without wind or tide,
   Moonless and sunless, the Mewlips hide.

     The cellars where the Mewlips sit
       Are deep and dank and cold
     With single sickly candle lit;
       And there they count their gold.

     Their walls are wet, their ceilings drip;
       Their feet upon the floor
     Go softly with a squish-flap-flip,
       As they sidle to the door.

     They peep out slyly; through a crack
       Their feeling fingers creep,
     And when they've finished, in a sack
       Your bones they take to keep.

Beyond the Merlock Mountains, a long and lonely
    road,
   Through the spider-shadows and the marsh of
    Tode,

And through the wood of hanging trees and the
    gallows-weed,
  You go to find the Mewlips — and the Mewlips
    feed.

10

OLIPHAUNT

Grey as a mouse,
Big as a house,
Nose like a snake,
I make the earth shake,
As I tramp through the grass;
Trees crack as I pass.
With horns in my mouth
I walk in the South,
Flapping big ears.
Beyond count of years
I stump round and round,
Never lie on the ground,
Not even to die.
Oliphaunt am I,
Biggest of all,
Huge, old, and tall.
If ever you'd met me,
You wouldn't forget me.

OLIPHAUNT

If you never do,
You won't think I'm true;
But old Oliphaunt am I,
And I never lie.

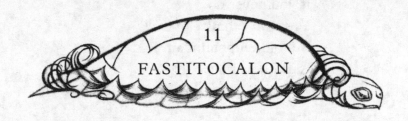

11

FASTITOCALON

Look, there is Fastitocalon!
An island good to land upon,
    Although 'tis rather bare.
Come, leave the sea! And let us run,
Or dance, or lie down in the sun!
        See, gulls are sitting there!
                Beware!
        Gulls do not sink.
There they may sit, or strut and prink:
Their part it is to tip the wink,
    If anyone should dare
    Upon that isle to settle,
Or only for a while to get
Relief from sickness or the wet,
    Or maybe boil a kettle.

Ah! foolish folk, who land on HIM,
And little fires proceed to trim
   And hope perhaps for tea!
It may be that His shell is thick,
He seems to sleep; but He is quick,
   And floats now in the sea
       With guile;
And when He hears their tapping feet,
Or faintly feels the sudden heat,
      With smile
      HE dives,
And promptly turning upside-down
He tips them off, and deep they drown,
   And lose their silly lives
    To their surprise.
     Be wise!
There are many monsters in the Sea,
But none so perilous as HE,
Old horny Fastitocalon,
Whose mighty kindred all have gone,
The last of the old Turtle-fish.
So if to save your life you wish
    Then I advise:
Pay heed to sailors' ancient lore,

Set foot on no uncharted shore!
　　Or better still,
Your days at peace on Middle-earth
　　In mirth
　　Fulfil!

12
CAT

The fat cat on the mat
   may seem to dream
of nice mice that suffice
   for him, or cream;
but he free, maybe,
   walks in thought
unbowed, proud, where loud
   roared and fought
his kin, lean and slim,
   or deep in den
in the East feasted on beasts
   and tender men.

The giant lion with iron
   claw in paw,
and huge ruthless tooth
   in gory jaw;
the pard dark-starred,

fleet upon feet,
that oft soft from aloft
leaps on his meat
where woods loom in gloom –
far now they be,
fierce and free,
and tamed is he;
but fat cat on the mat
kept as a pet,
he does not forget.

13

SHADOW-BRIDE

There was a man who dwelt alone,
  as day and night went past
he sat as still as carven stone,
  and yet no shadow cast.
The white owls perched upon his head
  beneath the winter moon;
they wiped their beaks and thought him dead
  under the stars of June.

There came a lady clad in grey
  in the twilight shining:
one moment she would stand and stay,
  her hair with flowers entwining.
He woke, as had he sprung of stone,
  and broke the spell that bound him;
he clasped her fast, both flesh and bone,
  and wrapped her shadow round him.

There never more she walks her ways
    by sun or moon or star;
she dwells below where neither days
    nor any nights there are.
But once a year when caverns yawn
    and hidden things awake,
they dance together then till dawn
    and a single shadow make.

14

THE HOARD

When the moon was new and the sun young
of silver and gold the gods sung:
in the green grass they silver spilled,
and the white waters they with gold filled.
Ere the pit was dug or Hell yawned,
ere dwarf was bred or dragon spawned,
there were Elves of old, and strong spells
under green hills in hollow dells
they sang as they wrought many fair things,
and the bright crowns of the Elf-kings.
But their doom fell, and their song waned,
by iron hewn and by steel chained.
Greed that sang not, nor with mouth smiled,
in dark holes their wealth piled,
graven silver and carven gold:
over Elvenhome the shadow rolled.

There was an old dwarf in a dark cave,
to silver and gold his fingers clave;
with hammer and tongs and anvil-stone
he worked his hands to the hard bone,
and coins he made, and strings of rings,
and thought to buy the power of kings.
But his eyes grew dim and his ears dull
and the skin yellow on his old skull;
through his bony claw with a pale sheen
the stony jewels slipped unseen.
No feet he heard, though the earth quaked,
when the young dragon his thirst slaked,
and the stream smoked at his dark door,
The flames hissed on the dank floor,
and he died alone in the red fire;
his bones were ashes in the hot mire.

There was an old dragon under grey stone;
his red eyes blinked as he lay alone.
His joy was dead and his youth spent,
he was knobbed and wrinkled, and his limbs bent
in the long years to his gold chained;
in his heart's furnace the fire waned.
To his belly's slime gems stuck thick,
silver and gold he would snuff and lick:

he knew the place of the least ring
beneath the shadow of his black wing.
Of thieves he thought on his hard bed,
and dreamed that on their flesh he fed,
their bones crushed, and their blood drank:
his ears drooped and his breath sank.
Mail-rings rang. He heard them not.
A voice echoed in his deep grot:
a young warrior with a bright sword
called him forth to defend his hoard.
His teeth were knives, and of horn his hide,
but iron tore him, and his flame died.

There was an old king on a high throne:
his white beard lay on knees of bone;
his mouth savoured neither meat nor drink,
nor his ears song; he could only think
of his huge chest with carven lid
where pale gems and gold lay hid
in secret treasury in the dark ground;
its strong doors were iron-bound.
The swords of his thanes were dull with rust,
his glory fallen, his rule unjust,
his halls hollow, and his bowers cold,
but king he was of elvish gold.

He heard not the horns in the mountain-pass,
he smelt not the blood on the trodden grass,
but his halls were burned, his kingdom lost;
in a cold pit his bones were tossed.

There is an old hoard in a dark rock,
forgotten behind doors none can unlock;
that grim gate no man can pass.
On the mound grows the green grass;
there sheep feed and the larks soar,
and the wind blows from the sea-shore.
The old hoard the Night shall keep,
while earth waits and the Elves sleep.

15

THE SEA-BELL

I walked by the sea, and there came to me,
 as a star-beam on the wet sand,
a white shell like a sea-bell;
 trembling it lay in my wet hand.
In my fingers shaken I heard waken
 a ding within, by a harbour bar
a buoy swinging, a call ringing
 over endless seas, faint now and far.

Then I saw a boat silently float
 on the night-tide, empty and grey.
'It is later than late! Why do we wait?'
 I leapt in and cried: 'Bear me away!'

It bore me away, wetted with spray,
 wrapped in a mist, wound in a sleep,
to a forgotten strand in a strange land.
 In the twilight beyond the deep

I heard a sea-bell swing in the swell,
    dinging, dinging, and the breakers roar
on the hidden teeth of a perilous reef;
    and at last I came to a long shore.
White it glimmered, and the sea simmered
    with star-mirrors in a silver net;
cliffs of stone pale as ruel-bone
    in the moon-foam were gleaming wet.
Glittering sand slid through my hand,
    dust of pearl and jewel-grist,
trumpets of opal, roses of coral,
    flutes of green and amethyst.
But under cliff-eaves there were glooming caves,
    weed-curtained, dark and grey;
a cold air stirred in my hair,
    and the light waned, as I hurried away.

Down from a hill ran a green rill;
    its water I drank to my heart's ease.
Up its fountain-stair to a country fair
    of ever-eve I came, far from the seas,
climbing into meadows of fluttering shadows:
    flowers lay there like fallen stars,
    and on a blue pool, glassy and cool,

like floating moons the nenuphars.
Alders were sleeping, and willows weeping
   by a slow river of rippling weeds;
gladdon-swords guarded the fords,
   and green spears, and arrow-reeds.

There was echo of song all the evening long
   down in the valley; many a thing
running to and fro: hares white as snow,
   voles out of holes; moths on the wing
with lantern-eyes; in quiet surprise
   brocks were staring out of dark doors.
I heard dancing there, music in the air,
   feet going quick on the green floors.
But wherever I came it was ever the same:
   the feet fled, and all was still;
never a greeting, only the fleeting
   pipes, voices, horns on the hill.

Of river-leaves and the rush-sheaves
   I made me a mantle of jewel-green,
a tall wand to hold, and a flag of gold;
   my eyes shone like the star-sheen.
With flowers crowned I stood on a mound,
   and shrill as a call at cock-crow

proudly I cried: 'Why do you hide?
   Why do none speak, wherever I go?
Here now I stand, king of this land,
   with gladdon-sword and reed-mace.
Answer my call! Come forth all!
   Speak to me words! Show me a face!'

Black came a cloud as a night-shroud.
   Like a dark mole groping I went,
to the ground falling, on my hands crawling
   with eyes blind and my back bent.
I crept to a wood: silent it stood
   in its dead leaves; bare were its boughs.
There must I sit, wandering in wit,
   while owls snored in their hollow house.
For a year and a day there must I stay:
   beetles were tapping in the rotten trees,
spiders were weaving, in the mould heaving
   puffballs loomed about my knees.

At last there came light in my long night,
   and I saw my hair hanging grey.
'Bent though I be, I must find the sea!
   I have lost myself, and I know not the way,
but let me be gone!' Then I stumbled on;

like a hunting bat shadow was over me;
in my ears dinned a withering wind,
    and with ragged briars I tried to cover me.
My hands were torn and my knees worn,
    and years were heavy upon my back,
when the rain in my face took a salt taste,
    and I smelled the smell of sea-wrack.

Birds came sailing, mewing, wailing;
    I heard voices in cold caves,
seals barking, and rocks snarling,
    and in spout-holes the gulping of waves.
Winter came fast; into a mist I passed,
    to land's end my years I bore;
snow was in the air, ice in my hair,
    darkness was lying on the last shore.

There still afloat waited the boat,
    in the tide lifting, its prow tossing.
Weary I lay, as it bore me away,
    the waves climbing, the seas crossing,
passing old hulls clustered with gulls
    and great ships laden with light,
coming to haven, dark as a raven,
    silent as snow, deep in the night.

Houses were shuttered, wind round them muttered,
    roads were empty. I sat by a door,
and where drizzling rain poured down a drain
    I cast away all that I bore:
in my clutching hand some grains of sand,
    and a sea-shell silent and dead.
Never will my ear that bell hear,
    never my feet that shore tread,
never again, as in sad lane,
    in blind alley and in long street
ragged I walk. To myself I talk;
    for still they speak not, men that I mcet.

16

THE LAST SHIP

Fíriel looked out at three o'clock:
    the grey night was going;
far away a golden cock
    clear and shrill was crowing.
The trees were dark, and the dawn pale,
    waking birds were cheeping,
a wind moved cool and frail
    through dim leaves creeping.

She watched the gleam at window grow,
    till the long light was shimmering
on land and leaf; on grass below
    grey dew was glimmering.
Over the floor her white feet crept,
    down the stair they twinkled,
through the grass they dancing stepped
    all with dew besprinkled.

Her gown had jewels upon its hem,
    as she ran down to the river,
and leaned upon a willow-stem,
    and watched the water quiver.
A kingfisher plunged down like a stone
    in a blue flash falling,
bending reeds were softly blown,
    lily-leaves were sprawling.

A sudden music to her came,
    as she stood there gleaming
with free hair in the morning's flame
    on her shoulders streaming.
Flutes there were, and harps were wrung,
    and there was sound of singing,
like wind-voices keen and young
    and far bells ringing.

A ship with golden beak and oar
    and timbers white came gliding;
swans went sailing on before,
    her tall prow guiding.
Fair folk out of Elvenland
    in silver-grey were rowing,

and three with crowns she saw there stand
   with bright hair flowing.

With harp in hand they sang their song
   to the slow oars swinging:
'Green is the land, the leaves are long,
   and the birds are singing.
Many a day with dawn of gold
   this earth will lighten,
many a flower will yet unfold,
   ere the cornfields whiten.'

'Then whither go ye, boatmen fair,
   down the river gliding?
To twilight and to secret lair
   in the great forest hiding?
To Northern isles and shores of stone
   on strong swans flying,
by cold waves to dwell alone
   with the white gulls crying?'

'Nay!' they answered. 'Far away
   on the last road faring,
leaving western havens grey,
   the seas of shadow daring,

we go back to Elvenhome,
　　where the White Tree is growing,
and the Star shines upon the foam
　　on the last shore flowing.

'To mortal fields say farewell,
　　Middle-earth forsaking!
In Elvenhome a clear bell
　　in the high tower is shaking.
Here grass fades and leaves fall,
　　and sun and moon wither,
and we have heard the far call
　　that bids us journey thither.'

The oars were stayed. They turned aside:
　　'Do you hear the call, Earth-maiden?
Fíriel! Fíriel!' they cried.
　　'Our ship is not full-laden.
One more only we may bear.
　　Come! For your days are speeding.
Come! Earth-maiden elven-fair,
　　our last call heeding.'

Fíriel looked from the river-bank,
　　one step daring;

then deep in clay her feet sank,
 and she halted staring.
Slowly the elven-ship went by
 whispering through the water:
'I cannot come!' they heard her cry.
 'I was born Earth's daughter!'

No jewels bright her gown bore,
 as she walked back from the meadow
under roof and dark door,
 under the house-shadow.
She donned her smock of russet brown,
 her long hair braided,
and to her work came stepping down.
 Soon the sunlight faded.

Year still after year flows
 down the Seven Rivers;
cloud passes, sunlight glows,
 reed and willow quivers
as morn and eve, but never more
 westward ships have waded
in mortal waters as before,
 and their song has faded.

Commentary

J.R.R. Tolkien in the grounds of Merton College, Oxford, reading
The Adventures of Tom Bombadil and Other Verses from the Red Book, 1968.
Photograph by John Wyatt.

PREFACE

Prior to *The Adventures of Tom Bombadil and Other Verses from the Red Book,* Tolkien had adopted the pose of an editor or translator of an old manuscript in his foreword to *Farmer Giles of Ham* (1949), in his prefatory note to the second edition of *The Hobbit* (1951), and in *The Lord of the Rings* (1954–5), in which he 'explained' that both that work and *The Hobbit* were drawn from the same source, the 'Red Book of Westmarch'. The title of the Red Book echoes those of medieval collections such as the 'Red Book of Hergest' and the 'Black Book of Carmarthen'; in the context of Tolkien's stories, it refers to the volumes mentioned in narrative near the end of *The Lord of the Rings* (bk. VI, ch. 9), one of which was given the title *The Downfall of the Lord of the Rings and the Return of the King.* In the Prologue to *The Lord of the Rings,* the Red Book is described as containing much besides the narrative of *The Lord of the Rings* proper.

Thus, in turn, the preface to the *Adventures of Tom Bombadil* collection mentions 'attached stories and chronicles', and poems 'on loose leaves' or 'written carelessly in margins and blank spaces'; and through this enlargement of an editorial fiction, the poems Tolkien wrote or revised for the 1962 book were given a history within the matter of Middle-earth, while the matter itself was enlarged through comments on Hobbit culture and notes on names and characters. The preface also serves, as Randel Helms said in *Tolkien's World* (1974), as a parody of textual scholarship, as self-parodying 'protection' against charges of bad poetry – because the verses are presented as the work of hobbits, not Tolkien's own – and as a means of establishing, if less seriously than in *The Lord of the Rings*, what Tolkien called Secondary Belief, in which the reader is brought willingly into the frame of a story.

We mention some of Tolkien's fictional points about specific poems in our discussions below, such as that the fifth selection, *The Man in the Moon Stayed Up Too Late*, is said to have been composed by Bilbo Baggins, hero of *The Hobbit*. Others are said to be by Sam Gamgee, or 'SG', or by Frodo Baggins, from *The Lord of the Rings*. The only poem in the collection not cited in the preface, for whatever reason there may have been, is *The Mewlips*.

Tolkien touches briefly in the preface on the 'strange words' and 'rhyming and metrical tricks' of some of the poems ('of hobbit origin'). In our discussions, we have glossed the more unusual or less common words, as they seem to us, while the reader, especially if the poems are read aloud, will easily detect many different rhyme patterns with occasional clever variations. Some, like the title poem, have straightforward rhyming couplets (AABB), while others are more elaborate; some (such as *Errantry*) have internal as well as external rhyme, and occasional alliteration; *The Hoard* makes use of *caesura*, a pause between each half-line, in the manner of Anglo-Saxon verse. The attributes of poetry of which Hobbits are said to be fond, and the act of verse-making, were entertaining to Tolkien himself. As he remarked to Margaret Carroux, translator of *The Lord of the Rings* into German, he was 'pleased by metrical devices and verbal skill (now out of fashion), and . . . amused by representing my imaginary historical period [of Middle-earth, in *The Hobbit* and *The Lord of the Rings*] as one in which these arts were delightful to poets and singers, and their audiences' (29 September 1968, Scull and Hammond, *The J.R.R.*

Tolkien Companion and Guide: Reader's Guide (2006), p. 768).

In Bilbo's 'scribble' near the beginning of the preface, a *weathercock* is the familiar wind-direction indicator in the shape of a bird (or *weathervane*, hence Tolkien's pun 'all is vane [vain]'). *Throstlecock*, or *throstle* for short, is an old-fashioned name for a song thrush.

The river-name *Serni* included in the first footnote of the preface was spelled *Sernui* in all earlier editions of this work; and in some printings, *Kiril* has been mis-spelled *Kirl*. *Serni*, however, is so spelled in all editions of *The Lord of the Rings*, and in later writings such as a 1969 letter by Tolkien to Pauline Baynes, advising her about names on her 1970 *Map of Middle-earth*; this spelling therefore is also used here. (And yet, as Carl F. Hostetter informs us, *Sernui* would be possible as an unattested adjectival formation *'stony' from *sarn* 'stone' in Tolkien's invented language Sindarin, on the model of *lithui* 'ashen'. In his late work *The Rivers and Beacon-hills of Gondor*, Tolkien names *Serni* with the same derivation.). In the text of *The Lord of the Rings*, *Kiril* is spelled *Ciril*, following Tolkien's late decision to spell Elvish names and words throughout with *C* rather than *K* (though still pronounced *K*), but it remained *Kiril* on the original *Lord of the Rings* maps, themselves produced late in the publishing process. In the *Bombadil* preface, *Kiril* perhaps should be *Ciril*, Tolkien's final preferred spelling and that used in most later versions or printings of the *Lord of the Rings* maps; but whereas *Sernui* is very likely a typographic error for *Serni*, for the preface Tolkien seems to have chosen to follow the *Lord of the Rings* map, as it stood in 1962, and it seemed right (if maybe inconsistent) to retain *Kiril* in the footnote.

In other respects, the preface as printed in this volume, and in all editions of *The Adventures of Tom Bombadil and Other Verses from the Red Book* since the second George Allen & Unwin printing in 1962, contains two errors, strictly speaking. In the first printing, *Cat* and *Fastitocalon* appeared in that order, but with the second printing, this order was reversed. References in the preface to these poems, numbers 11 and 12, however, were not altered (see further below, notes for *Fastitocalon*). Tolkien approved the change of order, but nowhere in his correspondence with Allen & Unwin is there discussion of whether to emend the preface to suit. In the absence of such evidence, and since Tolkien's prefatory comments on poems 11 and 12 apply (if not as aptly) even with the revised order, the original text has been allowed to stand.

THE ADVENTURES
OF TOM BOMBADIL

The first version of *The Adventures of Tom Bombadil* was published, under that title, in the *Oxford Magazine* for 15 February 1934:

> Old Tom Bombadil was a merry fellow;
> bright blue his jacket was, and his boots were
> yellow.
> He lived down under Hill; and a peacock's feather
> nodded in his old hat, tossing in the weather.
>
> Old Tom Bombadil walked about the meadows
> gathering the buttercups, a-chasing of the shadows,
> tickling the bumblebees a-buzzing in the flowers,
> sitting by the waterside for hours upon hours.
>
> There his beard dangled long down into the water:
> up came Goldberry, the Riverwoman's daughter;

pulled Tom's hanging hair. In he went a-wallowing
under the waterlilies, bubbling and a-swallowing.

'Hey! Tom Bombadil, whither are you going?'
said fair Goldberry. 'Bubbles you are blowing,
frightening the finny fish and the brown water-rat,
startling the dabchicks, drowning your feather-hat!'

'You bring it back again, there's a pretty maiden!'
said Tom Bombadil; 'I do not care for wading!
Go down! Sleep again, where the pools are shady
far below willow-roots, little water-lady!'

Back to her mother's house in the deepest hollow
swam young Goldberry; but Tom, he would not
     follow.
On knotted willow-roots he sat in sunny weather
drying his yellow boots and his draggled feather.

Up woke Willow-man, began upon his singing,
sang Tom fast asleep under branches swinging;
in a crack caught him tight: quiet it closed together,
trapped Tom Bombadil, coat and hat and feather.

'Ha! Tom Bombadil, what be you a-thinking,
peeping inside my tree, watching me a-drinking
deep in my wooden house, tickling me with feather,
dripping wet down my face like a rainy weather?'

'You let me out again, Old Man Willow!
I am stiff lying here; they're no sort of pillow,
your hard crooked roots. Drink your river water!
Go back to sleep again, like the River-daughter!'

Willow-man let him loose, when he heard him
        speaking;
locked fast his wooden house, muttering and
        creaking,
whispering inside the tree. Tom, he sat a-listening.
On the boughs piping birds were chirruping and
        whistling.
Tom saw butterflies quivering and winking;
Tom called the conies out, till the sun was sinking.

Then Tom went away. Rain began to shiver,
round rings spattering in the running river.
Clouds passed, hurrying drops were falling
        helter-skelter;
old Tom Bombadil crept into a shelter.

Out came Badger-brock with his snowy forehead
and his dark blinking eyes. In the hill he quarried
with his wife and many sons. By the coat they
    caught him,
pulled him inside the hole, down their tunnels
    brought him.

Inside their secret house, there they sat
    a-mumbling:
'Ho! Tom Bombadil, where have you come
    tumbling,
bursting in the front-door? Badgerfolk have caught
    you:
you'll never find it out, the way that we have
    brought you!'

'Now, old Badger-brock, do you hear me talking?
You show me out at once! I must be a-walking.
Show me to your backdoor under briar-roses;
then clean grimy paws, wipe your earthy noses!
Go back to sleep again on your straw pillow
like fair Goldberry and Old Man Willow!'

Then all the Badgerfolk said 'We beg your pardon!'
showed Tom out again to their thorny garden,

went back and hid themselves a-shivering and
    a-shaking,
blocked up all their doors, earth together raking.

Old Tom Bombadil hurried home to supper,
unlocked his house again, opened up the shutter,
let in the setting sun in the kitchen shining,
watched stars peering out and the moon climbing.

Dark came under Hill. Tom, he lit a candle,
up-stairs creaking went, turned the door handle.
'Hoo! Tom Bombadil, I am waiting for you
just here behind the door! I came up before you.
You've forgotten Barrow-wight dwelling in the old
    mound
up there a-top the hill with the ring of stones
    round.
He's got loose to-night: under the earth he'll take
    you!
Poor Tom Bombadil, pale and cold he'll make you!'

'Go out! Shut the door, and don't slam it after!
Take away gleaming eyes, take your hollow
    laughter!
Go back to grassy mound, on your stony pillow

lay down your bony head, like Old Man Willow,
like young Goldberry, and Badgerfolk in burrow!
Go back to buried gold and forgotten sorrow!'

Out fled Barrow-wight, through the window flying,
through yard, over wall, up the hill a-crying,
past white drowsing sheep, over leaning stone-rings,
back under lonely mound, rattling his bone-rings.

Old Tom Bombadil lay upon his pillow
sweeter than Goldberry, quieter than the Willow,
snugger than Badgerfolk, or the barrow-dwellers;
slept like a hummingtop, snored like a bellows.

He woke up in morning-light, whistled like a
        starling,
sang 'come, derry-dol, merry-dol, my darling!';
clapped on his battered hat, boots and coat and
        feather,
opened the window wide to the sunny weather.

Old Tom Bombadil was a clever fellow;
bright blue his jacket was, and his boots were
        yellow.
None ever caught old Tom, walking in the meadows

winter and summer-time, in the lights and shadows,
down dale, over hill, jumping over water —
but one day Tom he went and caught the
     River-daughter,
in green gown, flowing hair, sitting in the rushes,
an old song singing fair to birds upon the bushes.

He caught her, held her fast! Water-rats went
     scuttering,
reeds hissed, herons cried; and her heart was
     fluttering.
Said Tom Bombadil: 'Here's my pretty maiden!
You shall come home with me! The table is all
     laden:
yellow cream, honeycomb, white bread and butter;
roses at window-pane peeping through the shutter.
You shall come under Hill — never mind your
     mother
in her deep weedy pool: there you'll find no lover!'

Old Tom Bombadil had a merry wedding
crowned all in buttercups, his old feather shedding;
his bride with forgetmenots and flaglilies for
     garland,
robed all in silver-green. He sang like a starling,

hummed like a honeybee, lilted to the fiddle,
clasping his river-maid round her slender middle.

Lamps gleamed within his house, and white was
    the bedding;
in the bright honey-moon Badgerfolk came
    treading,
danced down under Hill, and Old Man Willow
tapped, tapped at window-pane, as they slept on
    the pillow;
on the bank in the reeds Riverwoman sighing
heard old Barrow-wight in his mound crying.

Old Tom Bombadil heeded not the voices,
taps, knocks, dancing feet, all the nightly noises;
slept till the sun arose, then sang like a starling:
'Hey! come, derry-dol, merry-dol, my darling!'
sitting on the doorstep chopping sticks of willow,
while fair Goldberry combed her tresses yellow.

In *The Return of the Shadow* (1988, pp. 115–16),
Christopher Tolkien printed a short poem, or part of
a poem (in five stanzas), which his father labelled the
'germ of Tom Bombadil so evidently [written] in mid
1930s'. This text begins:

(Said I)
'Ho! Tom Bombadil
    Whither are you going
With John Pompador
    Down the River rowing?'

Both text and note, however, are said by Christopher Tolkien to have been written 'certainly quite late' – late enough that the author was looking back over enough distance of time to state 'mid 1930s', presumably based on the date of publication of *The Adventures of Tom Bombadil* in the *Oxford Magazine*. It is a puzzling piece: if the manuscript is late, but the text is the 'germ of Tom Bombadil' in the sense of the origin of the poem (or of the character, or both), it must be a copy of a still earlier manuscript, and how early that document may have been produced, no one can say. To complicate the history still further, Tolkien wrote out excerpts of *The Adventures of Tom Bombadil* at least five times in an 'Elvish' script which has been dated to *c.* 1931. The 'germ', then, had to be written earlier than these. But also, the content and form of the 'germ' are found in development not in *The Adventures of Tom Bombadil*, but in its 'sequel', *Bombadil Goes Boating*.

Although the 1934 version of the poem is very similar to that published in *The Adventures of Tom Bombadil and Other Verses from the Red book*, there are numerous small differences. Most notably, in the earlier poem Tom wears a peacock's feather, rather than one from a swan's wing as in the 1962 revision or 'a long blue feather' as in *The Lord of the Rings* (bk. I, ch. 6; see further, our notes for *Bombadil Goes Boating*); in the tenth stanza, Tom calls *conies* (rabbits) out, presumably to play; and there are no references to the river Withywindle, since Tom in the original poem had no connection with Middle-earth, but rather was the 'spirit of the (vanishing) Oxford and Berkshire countryside' (letter to Stanley Unwin, 16 December 1937, *Letters*, p. 26). In the final stanza in the *Oxford Magazine*, 'derry-dol' is printed 'derry-rol', which seems a likely error and is emended in the text given above.

The characters of Tom Bombadil, Goldberry, Old Man Willow, and the Barrow-wight therefore were at hand in the 1934 poem for Tolkien to reuse when he came to write *The Lord of the Rings*. There (as finally published) Tom again wears 'an old battered hat', 'great yellow boots', and 'a blue coat', and sings often in rhyming couplets. There also, again following description in the poem, Goldberry's gown is green, with a belt 'shaped like a chain of flag-lilies set with the pale-blue eyes of forget-me-nots' (bk. I, ch. 6–7).

As Tolkien revised the *Oxford Magazine* poem for the 1962 collection, in a transitional version (Bodleian Library, Oxford, MS Tolkien 19, ff. 6–9) Tom briefly wore a broad silver belt buckle, and the poem finished with an extra couplet: 'Old Tom Bombadil lived in merry laughter / with his wife under Hill there for ever after!' The 1962 version adds a green *girdle* (belt) and leather breeches to Tom's wardrobe; and as mentioned above, it changes the source of his feather, Tolkien having decided that a peacock feather was 'unsuitable to' *The Lord of the Rings* but that one from a swan increased 'the riverishness' of the poem (letter to Pauline Baynes, 1 August 1962, *Letters*, p. 318). Tom and company were now, as in *The Lord of the Rings*, explicitly within lands known to Hobbits. Tolkien says in the *Bombadil* preface that the poem 'evidently' came from Buckland (on the east border of the Shire, as the boundaries stood at the start of *The Lord of the Rings*). *The Adventures of Tom Bombadil* is 'made up of various hobbit-versions of legends concerning Bombadil', who was regarded as benevolent, 'mysterious maybe and unpredictable but nonetheless comic'. The *Withywindle*, as described by Tolkien in his *Nomenclature of The Lord of the Rings*

(*The Lord of the Rings: A Reader's Companion*, p. 779), is 'a winding river bordered by willows (withies)', its name 'modelled on *withywind*, a name of the convolvulus or bindweed'. In the poem, the river runs from a 'grassy *well*', or spring, into a *dingle* or deep wooded valley.

Goldberry, the 'River-woman's daughter' (in the 1934 version, 'Riverwoman'), was carried over into the 1962 poem without further explanation, though her character is notably enlarged in *The Lord of the Rings*. Both she and her mother, their nature and place in the scheme of Tolkien's mythology, have been the subject of much discussion, but (as for the questions surrounding Tom Bombadil) without definitive resolution. In the poem, where Goldberry pulls Tom into the river by his beard, she resembles traditional water-sprites or nixies, sometimes accused of pulling humans into a river or lake to drown; in *The Lord of the Rings*, she is portrayed more as a nature spirit, related to seasonal change.

The poem episode of Old Man Willow catching Tom in a crack is echoed in *The Lord of the Rings* as Willow-man similarly traps Merry and Pippin. Under Tom's protection, the hobbits are advised to 'heed no nightly noise! Fear no grey willow!' just as Tom himself, in the poem, 'heeded not the voices, / taps, knocks, dancing feet, all the nightly noises'. Like Tom and Goldberry, the character of Old Man Willow grew in the later story: 'his song and thought ran through the woods and spread like fine root-threads in the ground, and invisible twig fingers in the air, till it had under its dominion nearly all the trees of the Forest from the Hedge to the Downs' (bk. I, ch. 7). According to Humphrey Carpenter in his *Biography*, Tolkien once said that the idea of Old Man Willow shutting someone up in a crack probably came in part from gnarled trees as distinctively drawn by the illustrator Arthur Rackham.

The *dabchicks* Goldberry accuses Tom of frightening are examples of a small waterbird, a grebe, with a long neck and short tail. The compound *Badger-brock* is simply a doubled word: *brock* is another name for 'badger'. In the revised poem, the badgers pull Tom 'inside their *earth*', a word for a badger's underground home which is typically lined with straw, hay, or grass; in the 1934 version, Tom is pulled more simply 'inside the hole'. A badger's earth, or sett, typically has multiple tunnels and several exits, hence references in the poem to 'the front-door' (where Tom takes shelter from the rain), 'backdoor', and 'all their doors'. In *The Lord of the Rings*, Tom tells the hobbits 'an absurd story about badgers and their queer ways' (bk. I, ch. 7).

A *barrow-wight* is an unearthly creature which inhabits a *barrow*, or burial mound. In Europe there is a long tradition of ancient burial mounds and stone circles; and in some of the barrows, the dead were interred with gold and other precious things. Wights are said in folklore to serve as sentinels of such treasure, thus Barrow-wight in the poem dwells (1962 version) 'in the old mound / up there on hill-top with the ring of stones round', and is bidden 'go back to buried gold'. There is also a tradition in Northern folk-belief in which the *draugr*, or living dead, haunted burial mounds (and elsewhere) and represented a threat to the truly living. In *The Lord of the Rings*, the Barrow-downs in which a wight entraps the four hobbits are given a history from the early days of Middle-earth, while the wight itself is an evil spirit who came to the mounds some two hundred years earlier, as an agent of the Witch-king of Angmar. The *bone-rings* the banished wight of the poem rattles in his 'lonely mound' are perhaps rings made from bone, of the sort sometimes found in burials; in *The Lord of the Rings*, Tom speaks of barrow-wights who 'walked in the hollow places with a clink of rings on cold fingers' (bk. I, ch. 7).

It is remarkable that Tom sends Goldberry, Old Man Willow, the badgers, and Barrow-wight to sleep before he himself sleeps, like a *humming-top* (1934 *humming-top*), a variation on the adage 'slept like a top', or very soundly, like a spinning top when it is at its steadiest.

BOMBADIL GOES BOATING

We have already mentioned that at some late date, Tolkien labelled a short text 'germ of Tom Bombadil so evidently [written] in mid 1930s'. We now give this in full:

> (Said I)
> 'Ho! Tom Bombadil
>   Whither are you going
> With John Pompador
>   Down the River rowing?'
>
> (Said he)
> 'Through Long Congleby,
>   Stoke Canonicorum,
> Past King's Singleton
>   To Bumby Cocalorum —

To call Bill Willoughby
　　Whatever he be doing
And ax Harry Larraby
　　What beer he is a-brewing.'

　　　　(And he sang)
'Go, boat! Row! The willows are a-bending,
　　reeds are leaning, wind is in the grasses.
Flow, stream, flow! The ripples are unending;
　　green they gleam, and shimmer as it passes.

Run, fair Sun, through heaven all the morning,
　　rolling golden! Merry is our singing!
Cool the pools, though summer be a-burning;
　　in shady glades let laughter run a-ringing!'

The names *John Pompador*, *Bill Willoughby*, and *Harry Larraby* appear to have no historical or literary significance, but suit the rhythm of the verses. The place-names in the second stanza serve a similar purpose. Of these, however, Christopher Tolkien in *The Return of the Shadow* has identified *Stoke Canonicorum* as the medieval name of the present Stoke Canon in Devonshire; but if *Long Congleby*, *King's Singleton*, and *Bumby Cocalorum* are (or were) also genuine names, we have not found them in Eilert Ekwall's dictionary of English place-names (1960 edn.) or any other references. Nonetheless, they have the *appearance* of genuine place-names, and incorporate common elements, such as *Long* from Old English *lang*, referring to the length of a piece of land, and *-by* from Old Norse *býr*, *boer*, Old Danish or Old Swedish *by*, denoting a village or homestead. Ekwall notes towns named *Singleton* with various possible etymologies, and *King's* appears both as a separate name element or in combination (as in *Kingston*). *Bumby* is a dialect word for 'marshy land, quagmire', and a *cocalorum*, or *cockalorum*, is a self-important little man. (Christopher Tolkien has told us privately that his father often used the word *cockalorum*, possibly to mean 'absurd, elaborate fuss'.) *Ax* is here a dialect form of 'ask'.

'The germ of Tom Bombadil' evolved at length into *Bombadil Goes Boating*, which had no published form before it appeared in the *Bombadil* collection in 1962. Tolkien developed the poem through at least ten versions as well as fragmentary workings (Bodleian Library, MS Tolkien 19, ff. 10–28, 37–40), calling it variously *The Fliting of Tom Bombadil*, *The Merry Fliting of Tom Bombadil*, and *The Adventures of Tom Bombadil II: The Merry Fliting* before settling on its less recondite final title. *Fliting*, from the Old English for 'strive' or 'quarrel', refers to a contest of insults, often in verse. Examples are found in Northern and medieval literature, for instance in the exchange in *Beowulf* between Beowulf and Unferth before the former faces Grendel. This indeed is the thread which runs through *Bombadil Goes Boating*, in which Tom is scolded by the willow-wren, the kingfisher, the otter, the swan, the 'little folk of Hays-end and Breredon', and Farmer Maggot, and gives back as good as he gets. Violent though the encounters may seem, in truth – and arrows in his hat notwithstanding – the many threats given or received by Tom are made in good humour. Tolkien says in the preface to the collection: 'Tom's raillery is here turned in jest upon his friends, who treat it with amusement (tinged with fear)'.

Early in the development of the poem, Tolkien extended the dialogue of the original three stanzas, so that Tom is asked a question in the first, replies in the second, is asked in the third to tell Bill Willoughby to mind what he is doing and to ask Harry Larraby about his beer, and replies again in a new fourth stanza, to the effect that (as far as Tom is concerned) Bill can do whatever he pleases, and there is no beer (brewed by Harry) as good as can be found 'Under-hill' (MS

Tolkien 19, f. 11). Tolkien soon omitted the initial dialogue, however, and introduced a new first stanza in which Tom decides to mend his boat and row down the river. The remainder of the poem grew until it became the longest of those in the *Bombadil* volume and contained the most complex vocabulary and allusions.

Bombadil Goes Boating begins in autumn, when the year 'was turning brown'. Tom having caught a falling leaf from a beech tree, he expresses a folk-belief that good luck follows catching a leaf before it reaches the ground. Some say that doing so brings a happy day, or month, or even twelve months of happiness; Tom takes his 'happy day' at once. He repairs his boat and journeys down the *withy-stream*, that is, the Withywindle, the river of the earlier poem (and *The Lord of the Rings*) bordered by willows (withies). Tolkien now plays on 'willow', first by introducing a *willow-wren* (the willow warbler) with its cry 'Whillo' (in draft, 'Willow', then 'Whillow'), then mentioning Willow-man (Old Man Willow) and the threat of a willow-spit, and at last the 'withy-willow-stream' in Tom's song. In the second and third stanzas, the willow-wren is a 'Little Bird' who offers to carry a message to Farmer Maggot, thus a proverbial 'little bird [who] told me' and a 'tell-tale'.

Tolkien glosses *Mithe* in the preface as 'the outflow of the Shirebourn'. The corresponding place-name element is derived from Old English *(ge)myðe* 'junction of streams'. Here, in the context of Middle-earth, the river Shirebourn flows into the Brandywine; in the preface, Tolkien adds that there 'was a landing-stage, from which a lane ran to Deephallow and so on to the Causeway road that went through Rushey and Stock', enlarging the geography of the Shire already established in *The Lord of the Rings*. The name *Shirebourn* is not derived from 'Shire' but from Old English *scïr* 'bright, clear, pure' + *burna* 'stream'.

Tom now *shaves* oars (makes or adjusts them with a spokeshave or drawing-knife), patches his *cockle-boat* (a small, shallow boat resembling a cockle-shell) – the kingfisher, and later the otter, deprecatingly calls it a 'tub' – and sets off through reed and *sallow-brake* (a clump or thicket of low-growing willows). *Hays-end*, where Tom knows 'little folk' (hobbits), is the end of the *hay* (an archaic word for 'hedge') or boundary fence that divides the Old Forest from Buckland; in the Shire map in *The Lord of the Rings*, it is marked at lower right (as 'Haysend'), at the junction of the rivers Brandywine and Withywindle.

After the willow-wren, a kingfisher teases Tom.

Although a 'gay lord' with brilliant blue plumage when on a bough, it lives 'in a *sloven* [untidy] house', a chamber tunnelled into a sandy bank and lined with disgorged fish bones and feces. T.A. Coward in *The Birds of the British Isles and Their Eggs*, a book Tolkien knew, describes the kingfisher's home as 'a running sewer of greenish liquid and decomposed fish [which] smells abominably' (1936 edn., p. 286). Coward also writes that 'when perched, facing the observer, [the kingfisher's] ruddy breast alone is seen' (p. 285), thus Tom's (exaggerated) statement 'though your breast be scarlet'. In drafts of the poem, Tolkien had written of a scarlet *crest*, but discovered that no variety of kingfisher likely to be seen in Britain would have that feature.

'Fisher-birds beak in air a-dangling / to show how the wind is set' refers to a folk-superstition described by Sir Thomas Browne in *Pseudoxia Epidemica* (1646), that if a kingfisher skin is hung by the bill, it turns like a weathercock to show from what quarter the wind is blowing. Tom makes the literal remark, 'that's an end of angling': the kingfisher would be dead, and no longer able to *angle* (though the bird does not, as this word denotes, fish with a hook and line). Tolkien wrote to Pauline Baynes that the allusion to Sir Thomas Browne was one of several 'donnish' details he included in

Bombadil Goes Boating, 'just [as] a private pleasure which I do not expect anyone to notice'. He found that the bird's name 'did not mean, as I had supposed, "a King that fishes". It was originally *the king's fisher*. That links the swan (traditionally the property of the King) with the fisher-bird; explains both their rivalry, and their special friendship with Tom: they were creatures who looked for the return of their rightful Lord, the true King' (1 August 1962, *Letters*, p. 319).

As we noted for the previous poem, Tom in *The Lord of the Rings* wears 'a long blue feather' (bk. I, ch. 6), rather than the peacock feather of the 1934 *Adventures of Tom Bombadil*, and in the 1962 revision Tolkien changed the feather's source from a peacock to a swan. This change was made also to allow for an episode in *Bombadil Goes Boating* which would tell retrospectively how Tom's feather came to be long and blue at the time he met the hobbits in the Old Forest: simply, that he found a stray feather from the kingfisher, lost as it left in a flash. (T.A. Coward writes, p. 285, that the king-fisher's flight is so rapid that 'a streak of blue as the bird vanishes round a bend is all that is often visible'.) The feather in Tom's hat was already blue in the early prose story of Tom in the days of King Bonhedig (see Appendix).

Critics before us have noticed in *Bombadil Goes Boating* (let alone the first part of *The Adventures of Tom Bombadil*) echoes of 'The River Bank', the first chapter of Kenneth Grahame's *Wind in the Willows* (1908). The most notable similarities are the introduction of the otter ('Whisker-lad'), with rings swirling around Tom's boat and bubbles quivering, and then his swift exit, 'Whoosh!' with 'river-water spraying': in Grahame's book, 'a streak of bubbles' travels 'along the surface of the water' before Otter appears to Mole and the Water Rat, and he leaves with 'a swirl of water and a "cloop!"'.

The otter's insult that 'Tom's gone mad as a coot with wooden legs' alludes to the saying *mad as a coot*, in which *coot* has the colloquial sense of a stupid, silly, or crazy person (rather than the water bird), while 'wooden legs' refers to the oars of Tom's cockle-boat. Tom's reply is more complex. He would give the otter's *fell* (pelt or skin) to Barrow-wights (see our notes for *The Adventures of Tom Bombadil*), who would *taw* it (make the skin into leather, using a chemical solution). The wights would then smother the otter in gold-rings, such that if his mother saw him, she would never know him unless by a whisker – an allusion to the story of 'Andvari's gold' in the medieval *Völsunga Saga* (or, with variation, in the *Elder Edda*) which may be summarized as follows. Otr (Otter), son of Hreidmar, could change his shape and often transformed into an otter to swim and fish. While in otter-form, he is seen by three of the Norse gods, one of whom kills him for his skin. But the gods are seized by Hreidmar and his other sons, who demand as compensation for Otr's death that his skin be covered with gold. This is done, until only a whisker remains exposed, and that in turn is concealed with a ring. Tolkien included a treatment of this story in his *Legend of Sigurd and Gudrún* (2009).

At the otter's departure appears 'Old Swan of *Elvet*-isle': *elvet* is an old word for 'swan', from Old English *elfetu*, surviving in place-names such as *Elvetham* in Hertfordshire. A *cob* is a male swan. Tom now alludes to the swan-wing feather he wore in *The Adventures of Tom Bombadil*, and in which it became 'worn by weather'. His insult, 'Could you speak a fair word . . . / long neck and dumb throat' reflects a folk-belief that swans are voiceless, or at least not musical, until just before death, when they sing a beautiful 'swan song'; but this is not true: even the so-called Mute Swan is not wholly without voice. 'If one day the King returns, in *upping* he may take you, / brand your yellow bill' refers to an annual census conducted since the twelfth century, of swans owned by the English crown, later with the Worshipful Company of Vintners and the Worshipful Company of Dyers. *Upping* means 'drive [swans] up or together', so that marks of ownership, in the form of nicks, could (formerly) be cut into the birds' bills; today, swans are given foot-rings with identification numbers.

Tom next comes to a *weir* or low dam built across the Withywindle. The meaning is evident from the need, at the end of the poem, to drag the cockle-boat 'over [the] weir' when being pushed upstream. The river rushes into the *reach* (an extended stretch of water), which leads Tom, 'spinning like a *windfall*' (in the manner of a twig or leaf blown down by the wind), to the *hythe* (or *hithe*, a landing-place) at Grindwall. In the *Bombadil* preface, Tolkien notes that '*Grindwall* was a small hythe on the north bank of the Withywindle; it was outside the Hay, and so was well watched and protected by a *grind* or fence extended into the water'.

Further in the same note, Tolkien writes that '*Breredon* (Briar Hill) [from Old English *brér* 'briar' + *dūn* 'hill'] was a little village on rising ground behind the hythe, in the narrow tongue between the end of the High Hay and the Brandywine'. Hobbits of Hays-end and Breredon now challenge Tom, insulting his facial hair as a "billy-beard', as if it were the beard of a billy-goat (male goat); in *The Hobbit,* Tolkien established that hobbits themselves have no beards. Tom, who lives in the Old Forest, is one of the 'Forest-folk'. His rejoinder 'fatbellies' refers to Hobbits' love of food and drink, though his own reputation for drinking has preceded him, if the beer barrels 'aint deep enough in Breredon' to *slake,* or satisfy, his thirst. *Orks* is a variant of *orcs* (goblins); the latter spelling is used in *The Lord of the Rings,* but the *-k* form appears in *Orkish.*

Although the 'little folk' make good their threat of three arrows in Tom's hat, the exchange ends in peace, as the hobbits carry him across the Brandywine by *wherry* (a light rowing-boat common on rivers and canals, distinct from the Norfolk wherry or sailing barge). At the Mithe Steps, or landing-stage, Farmer Maggot is not there to meet Tom, who now follows the Causeway road. The nearby village of *Rushey* (spelled 'Rushy' on the Shire map in *The Lord of the Rings*) is named for *rush* + Old Norse *-ey* 'isle', connoting a patch of hard land within marshes.

Maggot catches up and joins in the 'fliting', calling Tom a 'beggarman tramping in the *Marish*', the district of reclaimed marshland on the east side of the

Eastfarthing in the Shire (*marish* is an old form of *marsh*), and accusing him of seeking ale without intending to pay for it. Tom in reply calls his friend 'Muddyfeet', doubtless a severe insult to a marsh-dweller. (Tolkien states in the Prologue to *The Lord of the Rings* that while hobbits typically did not wear shoes, those of the Marish, like Farmer Maggot, had dwarf-boots for muddy weather.) Tom's 'penny-wise' counters Maggot's 'you've not a penny', and 'old farmer fat that cannot walk for wheezing, / cart-drawn like a sack' and 'tub-on-legs' insult Maggot's girth, pointing out that Tom has had to walk from the Mithe while the farmer drove a pony-cart. In Book I, Chapter 4 of *The Lord of the Rings*, Maggot is described as 'a broad thick-set hobbit with a round red face'.

At *cockshut light* (twilight) they pass by Rushey, 'could smell the *malting*' (the brewing of beer or ale, from malted grain), and proceed to Maggot's farm. Bamfurlong is familiar to readers of *The Lord of the Rings*, though it was named first in the *Bombadil* collection, and only in *The Lord of the Rings* from the 1967 second Allen & Unwin printing of the second edition. *Bamfurlong* has no particular meaning in the context of the story, but is an actual English place-name, probably derived from *bean* + *furlong*, indicating a strip of land usually reserved for beans. The name *Maggot* also is meant to be meaningless, but 'hobbit-like'; it does not refer to the English word for 'grub, larva'. The farmer is here given the honorific *goodman*, 'the master or male head of a household' (*Oxford English Dictionary*), and Mrs Maggot is similarly called *goodwife*.

A *hornpipe* is a solo dance traditionally associated with sailors. The *springle-ring* is a dance of Tolkien's own imagining, in which the participants often leap up – 'a pretty dance, but rather vigorous', he wrote in *The Lord of the Rings*, when in the middle of Bilbo's speech 'Master Everard Took and Miss Melilot Brandybuck got on a table and with bells in their hands began to dance the Springle-ring' (bk. I, ch. 1). *Springle* is a dialect word for 'nimble, active'. An *inglenook* is a chimney corner, a recess adjoining a fireplace.

In the *Bombadil* preface, Tolkien associates this poem, like *The Adventures of Tom Bombadil*, with Buckland because it shows 'more knowledge of that country, and of the Dingle, the wooded valley of the Withywindle, than any Hobbits west of the Marish were likely to possess'. The verses presenting Tom's visit to Bamfurlong tie *Bombadil Goes Boating* even more broadly to Hobbit lands, and to *The Lord of the Rings* in which it is established that Tom knows Farmer Maggot and exchanges news with him. The Barrow-downs are now mentioned again, and most notably, the Tower Hills: three hills with ancient towers, lying beyond the western borders of the Shire (until the Westmarch was added after the War of the Ring), and thus a great distance indeed for news to travel to the Marish.

'Queer tales from Bree' recalls the saying 'strange as news from Bree' in *The Lord of the Rings* (bk. I, ch. 9), with its meaning 'odd tidings'. The phrase 'talk at smithy, mill, and *cheaping* [market]', however, is drawn from the thirteenth-century *Ancrene Riwle* or rule for anchoresses (female religious recluses), on which Tolkien was a leading authority; there, as a caution against 'evil speech', the author quotes a proverb that 'from mill and cheaping, from smithy and from anchor-house [home of the anchoress] one hears the news'.

The 'tall Watchers by the Ford' are presumably, from *The Lord of the Rings*, Rangers (Men) of the North keeping watch, as at the crossing of the Brandywine at Sarn Ford. 'Shadows on the *marches*' (borderlands) echoes the Prologue to *The Lord of the Rings*: 'At the time when this story begins . . . there were many reports and complaints of strange persons and creatures prowling about the borders [of the Shire], or over them: the first sign that not all was as it should be. . . .' In one draft of the poem, the 'news' passed between Tom and Maggot also concerned: 'Dwarves going to and fro, Grey-elves from the Havens / on strange journeys in the Shire, gatherings of ravens, / rumours in whispering trees, shadows on the borders' (MS Tolkien 19, f. 22). In a letter to Pauline Baynes, Tolkien wrote that in contrast to *The Adventures of Tom Bombadil*, which he intended to be 'a hobbit-version of things long before the days of [the events of *The Lord of the Rings*]', *Bombadil Goes Boating* 'refers to the days of growing shadow, before Frodo set out' (1 August 1962, *Letters*, pp. 318–19); but in the preface to the collection, Tolkien states that the second poem 'was probably composed much later and after the visit of Frodo and his companions to the house of Bombadil'.

In its final stanzas, the 'actors' of the earlier verses reappear: the Old Swan, drawing Tom's boat by its *painter* (an attached line), the otter and his relations ('I'll go and tell my mother; / "Call all our kin to come') swimming around 'Willow-man's crooked roots' (Old Man Willow, thus along the Withywindle in the Old Forest as in *The Lord of the Rings*), the kingfisher on the bow, and the willow-wren on the *thwart* (the rower's seat). 'What's a coot without his legs' recalls otter's earlier taunt and refers to the oars left behind at Grindwall. But how did Tom return home without his boat? That must remain yet another mystery of Tom Bombadil.

ERRANTRY

Errantry is a revised version of a poem published, under the same title, in the *Oxford Magazine* for 9 November 1933:

> There was a merry passenger
> a messenger, a mariner:
> he built a gilded gondola
> to wander in, and had in her
> a load of yellow oranges
> and porridge for his provender;
> he perfumed her with marjoram
> and cardamom and lavender.
>
> He called the winds of argosies
> with cargoes in to carry him
> across the rivers seventeen
> that lay between to tarry him.

He landed all in loneliness
where stonily the pebbles on
the running river Derrilyn
goes merrily for ever on.
He wandered over meadow-land
to shadow-land and dreariness,
and under hill and over hill,
a rover still to weariness.

He sat and sang a melody
his errantry a-tarrying;
he begged a pretty butterfly
that fluttered by to marry him.
She laughed at him, deluded him,
eluded him unpitying;
so long he studied wizardry
and sigaldry and smithying.

He wove a tissue airy-thin
to snare her in; to follow in
he made him beetle-leather wing
and feather wing and swallow-wing.
He caught her in bewilderment
in filament of spider-thread;
he built a little bower-house,

a flower house, to hide her head;
he made her shoes of diamond
on fire and a-shimmering;
a boat he built her marvellous,
a carvel all a-glimmering;
he threaded gems in necklaces —
and recklessly she squandered them,
as fluttering, and wavering,
and quavering, they wandered on.

They fell to bitter quarrelling;
and sorrowing he sped away,
on windy weather wearily
and drearily he fled away.

He passed the archipelagoes
where yellow grows the marigold,
where countless silver fountains are,
and mountains are of fairy-gold.
He took to war and foraying
a-harrying beyond the sea,
a-roaming over Belmarie
and Thellamie and Fantasie.

He made a shield and morion
of coral and of ivory,
a sword he made of emerald,
and terrible his rivalry
with all the knights of Aerie
and Faërie and Thellamie.
Of crystal was his habergeon,
his scabbard of chalcedony,
his javelins were of malachite
and stalactite — he brandished them,
and went and fought the dragon-flies
of Paradise, and vanquished them.

He battled with the Dumbledores,
the Bumbles, and the Honeybees,
and won the Golden Honeycomb;
and running home on sunny seas
in ship of leaves and gossamer
with blossom for a canopy,
he polished up, and furbished up,
and burnished up his panoply.

He tarried for a little while
in little isles, and plundered them;
and webs of all the Attercops

he shattered them and sundered them —
Then, coming home with honeycomb
and money none, to memory
his message came and errand too!
In derring-do and glamoury
he had forgot them, journeying,
and tourneying, a wanderer.

So now he must depart again
and start again his gondola,
for ever still a messenger,
a passenger, a tarrier,
a-roving as a feather does,
a weather-driven mariner.

The versions of *Errantry* printed in this book have many differences of detail and phrasing, most notably from the point in the fourth stanza of the 1962 poem at which the mariner makes the butterfly 'soft pavilions / of lilies, and a bridal bed / of flowers and of thistle-down', and from the fifth stanza in the *Oxford Magazine* poem, where 'he built a little bower-house, / a flower house, to hide her head'. But they represent only two of many revisions in the poem's remarkably long and complex history. In a letter of 14 October 1966 to the composer Donald Swann (who would set the 1962 poem to music in his song cycle *The Road Goes Ever On*, published 1967), Tolkien said that *Errantry* 'was begun very many years ago, in an attempt to go on with the model that came unbidden into my mind: the first six lines, in which, I guess, *D'ye ken the rhyme to porringer* had a part' (quoted in *The Treason of Isengard* (1989), p. 85). As first identified independently by Alan Stokes and Neil Gaiman, 'D'ye ken the rhyme to porringer' refers to a Jacobite song about the Revolution of 1688, in which the Catholic King James II of England (James VII of Scotland) was deposed by his Protestant son-in-law, William of Orange:

> O what's the rhyme to porringer?
> Ken ye the rhyme to porringer?
> King James the Seventh had ae dochter
> [a daughter]
> And he ga'e [gave] her to an Oranger.

The song also inspired a nursery rhyme, beginning 'What is the rhyme for porringer?' (A *porringer* is a small bowl or vessel for eating porridge, soup, or the like.)

As he wrote to Donald Swann, Tolkien intended his poem to be

a piece of verbal acrobatics and metrical high-jinks . . .
for recitation with great variations of speed. It needs
a reciter or chanter capable of producing the words
with great clarity, but in places with great rapidity.
The 'stanzas' as printed [in the *Bombadil* volume]
indicate the speed-groups. In general these were
meant to begin at speed and slow down. Except the
last group, which was to begin slowly, and pick up at
errand too! and end at high speed to match the begin-
ning. Also of course the reciter was supposed at once
to begin repeating (at even higher speed) the begin-
ning, unless somebody cried 'Once is enough'. [*The
Treason of Isengard*, p. 85]

Elsewhere, Tolkien said that it was an elaboration on
the 'never-ending Tale' (*The Treason of Isengard*, p. 106).
The earliest extant version of *Errantry* evidently
is a fair copy, written without hesitation and with its
own set of differences from the *Oxford Magazine* and
Bombadil versions. This manuscript begins:

> There was a merry passenger,
> a messenger, an errander;
> he took a tiny porringer

and oranges for provender;
he took a little grasshopper
and harnessed her to carry him; . . .

The complete text may be found in *The Treason of Isengard* (ch. 5) as part of a lengthy analysis by Christopher Tolkien, with excerpts from four additional versions written before the poem was published in November 1933. That appearance in the *Oxford Magazine* is a convenient terminus, but the date of original composition remains uncertain. Tolkien is known to have read the poem to a group of Oxford undergraduates (the earliest 'Inklings') in the early 1930s, and in whole or in part, he wrote out the poem (with variations) at least three times in an 'Elvish' script which has been dated to *c.* 1931.

Much later, he learned that *Errantry* somehow had entered oral tradition, and that versions had circulated or been published without mention of the author. These bore out his view that in oral transmission 'hard' words (such as *sigaldry*) tend to be preserved, while more common words are altered and metre is often disturbed. The metre of *Errantry* was unusual, he told Rayner Unwin, 'depending on trisyllabic assonances or near-assonances, which is so difficult that except in this one example I have never been able to use it again – it just blew out in a single impulse' (22 June 1952, *Letters*, p. 162).

That 'impulse', however, gave rise also to the poem *Eärendil Was a Mariner*, which began as a variant of *Errantry*, even in its first version with the opening words 'There was a merry messenger', before taking a different course (likewise traced in *The Treason of Isengard*) until it became the song chanted by Bilbo at Rivendell in *The Lord of the Rings*, Book II, Chapter 1. In that line of development, *Errantry* became a modified account of the great sea-voyage of Eärendil from 'The Silmarillion', which ends with the mariner's transformation into a star, 'the Flammifer of Westernesse'.

Tolkien apparently foresaw that readers of the *Bombadil* collection would notice the similarity between *Errantry* and *Eärendil Was a Mariner*, for in its preface he calls *Errantry*

> an example of another kind [of poem] which seems to have amused Hobbits: a rhyme or story which returns to its beginning, and so may be recited until the hearers revolt. Several specimens are found in the Red Book, but the others are simple and crude. [*Errantry*] is much the longest and most elaborate.

It was evidently made by Bilbo. This is indicated by its obvious relationship to the long poem recited by Bilbo, as his own composition in the house of Elrond. In origin a 'nonsense rhyme', it is in the Rivendell version found transformed and applied, somewhat incongruously, to the high-elvish and Númenórean legends of Eärendil.

The mariner's *gondola* was drawn by illustrator Pauline Baynes as a fantastic ('gilded') elaboration on the craft found in Venetian canals, with unicorn figure-head and two barrels beneath the canopy, presumably *provender* (food, supplies); but *gondola* also has a less common meaning, 'a ship's boat; some kind of small war-vessel' (*Oxford English Dictionary*). *Marjoram, cardamom* (or *cardomon*), and *lavender* are aromatics, used in perfumes as well as cooking.

'Winds of argosies' would be those favourable to *argosies* or large merchant ships. *Derrilyn*, along with *Shadow-land, Belmarie, Thellamie, Fantasie, Aerie*, and *Faerie* (in 1933, *Faërie*), as well as *Paradise* and 'the archipelagoes / where yellow grows the marigold', are not meant to refer to particular places, only to the poet's fancy, and are convenient rhymes. In the preface, Tolkien notes that names such as *Derrilyn* and

Thellamie 'are mere inventions in the Elvish style, and are not in fact Elvish at all'.

Sigaldry is an old word for 'enchantment, sorcery', from Old English *sigalder* 'charm, incantation'; Middle English *sigaldrie* occurs in the *Ancrene Riwle* (see our notes for *Bombadil Goes Boating*). The practice of *smithying* (forging, working in metal) enters into the poem four verses later, with mention of a shield, helmet, sword, and the like.

In the 1933 poem only, *bower* is a poetic word for 'dwelling', especially one for a lady and of an idealized form ('a flower-house'). The shoes the mariner makes 'of diamond / on fire and a-shimmering' recall the flashing slippers of fishes' mail in *Princess Mee*; in the earliest manuscript, where he undertakes no special study (of sorcery) until later in the poem, the mariner makes the butterfly 'shoes of beetle-skin / with needles in to latch them with' (*The Treason of Isengard*, p. 86). A *carvel* (or *caravel*) is a small, fast ship.

Foray is 'to make a hostile or predatory incursion', and *harry* 'to persistently attack'. A *morion* is an open helmet; a *paladin*, a knight errant or champion; a *habergeon*, a sleeveless coat of armour; *chalcedony*, a type of quartz; *plenilune*, the time of the full moon; *malachite*, a bright green mineral; a *stalactite*, the spear-like

THE ADVENTURES OF TOM BOMBADIL

structure formed by mineral deposits dripping from the roofs of caves; and *dumbledor*, a dialect word for 'bumble-bee'. *Hummerhorn* seems to be a Tolkien invention, but in context with bumble-bees (Dumbledors) and Honeybees, it is presumably meant to be another 'humming' insect, such as a wasp or hornet. The prize of a *Golden Honeycomb* recalls the Golden Fleece from the Greek myth of Jason and the Argonauts.

Gossamer is a word for 'fine cobwebs'. The mariner *furbishes* and *burnishes* his *panoply*, that is, removes rust and polishes his armour. *Derring-do* means 'a display of courage or heroism', and *glamoury* 'enchantment, magic'. In the 1933 poem, the mariner shatters the webs of *Attercops* or spiders, a dialect word from Old English *attor* 'poison', which Tolkien would have seen in the thirteenth-century poem *The Owl and the Nightingale*, and which he used also in *The Hobbit*.

John D. Rateliff has pointed out interesting similarities between *Errantry* and Chaucer's 'Sir Thopas' in the *Canterbury Tales*. In that burlesque of the metrical romance, Thopas, a knight of Flanders, loves the elf-queen, but must do battle with a giant. Therefore he arms himself, in a manner reminiscent of Tolkien's mariner:

His jambeux were of quyrboilly,
His swerdes shethe of yvory,
His helm of latoun bright;
His sadel was of rewel boon,
His brydel as the sonne shoon,
Or as the moone light.

('His leg armour was of hardened leather [*cuir bouilli*], his sword's sheath of ivory, his helm was of bright latten [an alloy of copper, tin, and other metals]; his saddle was of ruel-bone [whale ivory], his bridle shone like the sun, or like moonlight.') Others have suggested that *Errantry*, with its 'pretty butterfly', fairy-gold, elven-knights, and the like, is a response by Tolkien to his views on 'the diminutive being, elf or fairy, . . . a literary business in which William Shakespeare and Michael Drayton played a part'. Drayton's *Nimphidia*, Tolkien wrote, singling out 'one of the worst [fairy-stories] ever written', 'is one ancestor of that long line of flower-fairies and fluttering sprites with antennae that I so disliked as a child, and which my children in their turn detested' (*On Fairy-Stories*, first published 1947, quoted from *The Monsters and the Critics and Other Essays* (1983), p. 111).

PRINCESS MEE

In 1924, while Reader in English Language at the
University of Leeds, Tolkien published a precursor to
Princess Mee, entitled *The Princess Ní*, in the collection
Leeds University Verse 1914–24:

> O! the Princess Ní,
> Slender is she:
> In gossamer shot with gold,
> And splintered pearls

> On threaded curls
> Of elfin hair, 'tis told,
> She is wanly clad;
> But with myriad

> Fireflies is she girdled,
> Like garnets red

In an amber bed,
While her silver slippers, curdled

With opals pale,
Are of fishes' mail —
How they slide on the coral floor! —
And over her frock

She wears a smock,
A feathery pinafore,
Of the down of ciders
With red money-spiders

Broidered here and there.
O! the Princess Ní,
Most slender is she,
And lighter than the air.

Although Tolkien came to deplore the idea of diminutive, 'elfin' beings – 'a murrain on Will Shakespeare and his damned cobwebs' (late 1951?, *Letters*, p. 143) – they featured in some of his earlier poems: the earliest extant manuscript of *The Princess Ni* is dated 9 July 1915. Here, however, the emphasis is less on the figure of the princess than on her raiment, which Tolkien describes in exquisite detail. As in *Errantry*, *gossamer* can be taken in its strict sense of 'fine cobwebs'. The princess is '*wanly* clad' (dressed in a pale garment), though with coloured decoration, and with silver slippers festooned with *opals* (pale or colourless silica) like milky curds. For a *smock* she wears a *pinafore* (both words refer to a loose protective overgarment) of *eider down* (soft feathers from an eider duck), embroidered with *money-spiders* (small spiders supposed to bring good luck). Goldberry in *The Lord of the Rings* herself wears shoes 'like fishes' mail' (bk. I, ch. 7). The name *Ní* is derived, maybe, from the Irish feminine patronymic, as in the mythic *Caitlín Ní Uallacháin* (Cathleen Ni Houlihan).

Princess Mee, written no later than 15 November 1961, preserves some of the tone and description of *The Princess Ní*. In the *Bombadil* preface, Tolkien classifies it among the 'nonsense' of the Red Book's 'marginalia', suggesting that it is no more than a hobbit's idea of an Elf-maiden, dancing on a pool of clear water while dressed in a 'woven coat' as light as the silken webs spun by moths and 'sewn with diamond dew'. In fact, the poem is quietly sophisticated, with its imagery of Princess Mee 'dancing toe to toe' with 'Princess Shee', its reversal of the final four lines to reflect the four preceding them, and its sad comment that none could discover how to find the mirror-world of the dancer's reflection.

More than one critic has described *Princess Mee* as a version of the myth of Narcissus, the youth doomed to love his own reflection but never to reach that other self mirrored in the water; in that respect, the character's name, *Mee*, is appropriately self-absorbed, but for the poem's purposes, it need be no more than a contrast with *Shee*.

Much of the imagery in *Princess Mee* – silver and light, dancing beneath the stars – is common in Tolkien's writing, and recalls most notably the dancing of Lúthien Tinúviel in 'The Silmarillion' (here from Canto 3 of *The Lay of Leithian*, in *The Lays of Beleriand* (1985), pp. 174–5):

> Her arms like ivory were gleaming,
> her long hair like a cloud was streaming,
> her feet atwinkle wandered roaming
> in misty mazes in the gloaming;
> and glowworms shimmered round her feet,
> and moths in moving garland fleet
> above her head went wavering wan —

and this the moon now looked upon,
uprisen slow, and round, and white,
above the branches of the night.

A *kerchief* could be a covering for the head or for the breast or shoulders, while a *kirtle* is a woman's gown or an outer petticoat. All of these are possible in the larger illustration of Princess Mee by Pauline Baynes, who seems to have hedged her bets.

THE MAN IN THE MOON
STAYED UP TOO LATE

The Man in the Moon Stayed Up Too Late is the title given to the poem in the *Bombadil* collection, where it is reprinted (with two slight revisions) from *The Lord of the Rings*, Book I, Chapter 9. It was first composed probably in the period 1919–20. The text of its original version may be found in *The Return of the Shadow*, pp. 145–7; a revision, with only minor differences, was published as follows in the Leeds journal *Yorkshire Poetry* for October–November 1923 as *The Cat and the Fiddle: A Nursery-Rhyme Undone and Its Scandalous Secret Unlocked*:

They say there's a little crooked inn
    Behind an old grey hill,
Where they brew a beer so very brown
The Man-in-the-Moon himself comes down,
    And sometimes drinks his fill.

And there the ostler has a cat
  Who plays a five-stringed fiddle;
Mine host a little dog so clever
He laughs at any joke whatever,
  And sometimes in the middle.

They also keep a horned cow,
  'Tis said, with golden hoofs;
But music turns her head like ale,
And makes her wave her tufted tail
  And dance upon the roofs.

But O! the row of silver dishes,
  And store of silver spoons:
For Sunday there's a special pair,
And these they polish up with care
  On Saturday afternoons.

The Man-in-the-Moon had drunk too deep;
  The ostler's cat was totty;
A dish made love to a Sunday spoon;
The little dog saw all the jokes too soon;
  And the cow was dancing-dotty.

The Man-in-the-Moon had another mug
 And fell beneath his chair,
And there he called for still more ale,
Though the stars were getting thin and pale,
 And the Dawn was on the stair.

The ostler said to his tipsy cat:
 'The white horses of the Moon,
They neigh and champ their silver bits,
But their master's been and drowned his wits,
 And the Sun will catch him soon.

Come play on your fiddle a hey-diddle-diddle,
 'Twill make him look alive.'
So the cat played a terrible drunken tune,
While the landlord shook the Man-in-the-Moon,
 And cried ''tis nearly five!'

They rolled him slowly up the hill
 And bundled him in the Moon;
And his horses galloped up in rear,
And the cow came capering like a deer,
 And the dish embraced the spoon.

The cat then suddenly changed the tune;
　　The dog began to roar;
　　　The horses stood upon their heads;
The guests all bounded upon their beds
　　And danced upon the floor.

The cat broke all his fiddle-strings;
　　The cow jumped over the Moon;
The little dog laughed to see such fun;
In the middle the Sunday dish did run
　　Away with the Sunday spoon.

The round Moon rolled off over the hill —
　　But only just in time,
For the Sun looked up with a fiery head,
And ordered everyone back to bed,
　　And the ending of the rhyme.

　　The rhyme that has come 'undone' or 'unlocked' is
one of the best known of English nursery rhymes:

Hey diddle diddle,
The cat and the fiddle,
The cow jumped over the moon;

The little dog laughed
To see such sport
And the dish ran away with the spoon.

But as first suggested by George Burke Johnston, Tolkien may have been inspired also by 'The True History of the Cat and the Fiddle' by George MacDonald in *At the Back of the North Wind* (1870), in which 'Hey Diddle Diddle' is combined with the traditional rhyme 'The Man in the Moon Came Down Too Soon' (see also our notes for Tolkien's poem of that title, below):

Hey, diddle, diddle!
The cat and the fiddle!
He played such a merry tune,
That the cow went mad
With the pleasure she had,
And jumped right over the moon.
But then, don't you see?
Before that could be,
The moon had come down and listened.
The little dog hearkened,
So loud that he barkened,
'There's nothing like it, there isn't.'

Hey, diddle, diddle!
Went the cat and the fiddle,
Hey diddle, diddle, dee, dee!
The dog laughed at the sport
Till his cough cut him short,
It was hey diddle, diddle, oh me!
And back came the cow
With a merry, merry low,
For she'd humbled the man in the moon,
The dish got excited,
The spoon was delighted,
And the dish waltzed away with the spoon.

Revised for *The Lord of the Rings*, *The Cat and the Fiddle* is sung by Frodo at the inn at Bree, and in that work, as in the *Bombadil* preface, it is said to have been composed by Bilbo Baggins. The *Lord of the Rings* poem differs from the version in the *Bombadil* volume at only two points: in the eighth stanza, 'The ostler said to his tipsy cat' reads (our emphasis) '*Then* the ostler said to his tipsy cat'; and in the tenth stanza, 'and a dish ran up with a spoon' reads 'and a dish ran up with *the* spoon'.

Ostler refers historically to a *hostler*, or *hosteler* (with silent *h*), one who runs a hostelry (or inn), later (and probably here) more specifically to a stableman or groom for guests' horses. The ostler's mention of white horses may be an echo of those sometimes shown in art to draw the chariot of the moon-goddess Selene (Luna). In *The Cat and the Fiddle*, *totty* means 'unsteady, dizzy'; here it rhymes with *dotty*, also 'unsteady' but figuratively 'silly'. In *The Lord of the Rings*, Tolkien glosses the female pronouns in Frodo's song which refer to the Sun, explaining that 'Elves (and Hobbits) always refer to the Sun as She'.

THE MAN IN THE MOON
CAME DOWN TOO SOON

The second 'Man in the Moon' poem in this book is a revision of *Why the Man in the Moon Came Down Too Soon,* one of three works (with *Enigmata Saxonica Nuper Inventa Duo* and *Tha Eadigan Saelidan: The Happy Mariners*) which Tolkien contributed in June 1923 to *A Northern Venture: Verses by Members of the Leeds University English School Association*:

> The Man in the Moon had silver shoon
>   And his beard was of silver thread;
> He was girt with pale gold and inaureoled
>   With gold about his head.
> Clad in silken robe in his great white globe
>   He opened an ivory door
> With a crystal key, and in secrecy
>   He stole down the lucent floor;

Down a filigree stair of spidery hair
    He slipped in gleaming haste,
And laughed with glee to be merry and free,
    And faster he earthward raced —
He was tired of his pearls and diamond twirls,
    Of his pallid minaret
Dizzy and white at its lunar height
    In a world of silver set;

And adventured this peril for ruby and beryl
    And emerald and sapphire,
And all lustrous gems for new diadems,
    Or to blazon his pale attire.
He was lonely too with nothing to do
    But to stare at the golden world,
Or strain for the hum that would distinctly come
    As it gaily past him whirled.

At plenilune in his argent moon
    He had wearily longed for fire:
Not the limpid lights of wan selenites,
    But a red terrestrial pyre
With impurpurate glows of crimson and rose
    And leaping orange tongue;

For great seas of blues and the passionate hues
  When a dancing dawn is young;

For the meadowy ways like chrysoprase
  At topaz eve — and then
How he longed for the mirth of the populous Earth
  And the sanguine blood of men;
And coveted song and laughter long,
  And viands hot, and wine,
Eating pearly cakes of light snowflakes
  And drinking thin moonshine.

He twinkled his feet as he thought of the meat,
  Of the punch and the peppery stew,
Till he tripped unaware on his slanting stair,
  And fell like meteors do;
As the whickering sparks in splashing arcs
  Of stars blown down like rain
From his laddery path took a foamy bath
  In the Ocean of Almain;

And began to think, lest he melt and sink,
  What in the moon to do,
When a Yarmouth boat found him far afloat,
  To the mazement of the crew

Caught in their net all shimmering wet
    In a phosphorescent sheen
Of bluey whites and opal lights
    And delicate liquid green.

With the morning fish — 'twas his regal wish —
    They packed him to Norwich town
To get warm on gin in a Norfolk inn,
    And dry his watery gown.
Though canorous spells from the musical bells
    Of the city's fifty towers
Shouted the news of his lunatic cruise
    In the early morning hours,

No hearths were laid, not a breakfast made,
    And no one would sell him gems.
He found ashes for fire, and his gay desire
    For chorus and brave anthems
Met snores instead with all Norfolk abed;
    And his round heart nearly broke,
More empty and cold than above of old,
    Till he bartered his faerie cloak

For a kitchen nook by a smoky cook,
    And his belt of gold for a smile,

And a priceless jewel for a bowl of gruel —
    A sample cold and vile
Of the proud plum-porridge of Anglian Norwich —
    He arrived so much too soon
For unusual guests on adventurous quests
    From the mountains of the Moon.

Shoon is the archaic plural of *shoe* – in these, the Man in the Moon *twinkled* his feet (moved them lightly and rapidly). His head is *inaureoled*, as if with a halo or heavenly crown. The floor is *lucent* (shining, luminous), the *minaret* (a slender tower, here divorced from its meaning as the turret of a mosque) is *pallid* or pale, like the *limpid* (clear) lights of *wan* (pale) *selenites* (precious stones, white and transparent; *selen-* is Greek 'moon'). Tolkien's moon is white, ivory, or crystal, 'a world of silver set', a place of light without colour. Against this, the 'golden' earth is a temptation, with its rich mineral colours – ruby and beryl, emerald and sapphire, *chrysoprase* (chalcedony) and topaz, 'lustrous gems for new *diadems*' (crowns or headbands) or to *blazon* (display prominently on) the Man in the Moon's 'pale attire' – its fire with *impurpurate* (purple) glows and 'leaping orange tongue', its blue seas, and its colourful dawn. *Plenilune* (the time of full moon) and *argent* (silver) are words which Tolkien thought beautiful before they are even understood (see his comments to Jane Neave, *Letters*, p. 310).

Why the Man in the Moon Came Down Too Soon 'explains' the well-known (with variations) English nursery rhyme:

> The man in the moon
> Came down too soon,
> And asked his way to Norwich;
> He went by the south,
> And burnt his mouth
> With supping cold plum porridge.

In Tolkien's poem, the Man in the Moon falls, like sparks *whickering* (making a sound like something rushing through the air) and down a *filigree* stair (like delicate jewel work), into 'the Ocean of Almain', the North Sea (*Almain* is an older English name for Germany, and the North Sea has been called the 'German Ocean'). Into these waters juts the English county of Norfolk in the region of East Anglia, with its capital at Norwich; East Anglia is so called because it was settled by Angles, thus 'Anglian Norwich' in the final stanza. From medieval times, Norwich has been a major city in England, with many churches and (latterly) two cathedrals, a place of many towers whose bells could well cast *canorous* (melodious, resonant) spells. The 'Yarmouth boat' whose crew find the Man is out of Great Yarmouth, a town south of Norwich and once a major fishing port. The gruel he buys at a dear price, a 'cold and vile' sample of plum-porridge (see below), and his equally cold reception by those folk of Norwich awake at an early hour are not the *sanguine* (warm, cheerful) men and hot *viands* (foods) the Man desires.

The earliest workings of *Why the Man in the Moon Came Down Too Soon* are dated 10–11 March 1915 and subtitled *An East Anglian Phantasy*. Tolkien later omitted the subtitle and added a foretitle, *A Faërie*, as well as a title in Old English, *Se Móncyning* ('The Moon-king'). Another version of the poem, following that in *A Northern Venture* but still retaining (indeed, adding) references to Norwich, was published in *The Book of Lost Tales, Part One*, pp. 204–6. Possibly in mid-May 1915, Tolkien wrote four lines from the original poem (from 'He was tired of his pearls . . .') in the notebook he called *The Book of Ishness*, accompanied by a watercolour, 'Illustr[ation]: To "Man in the Moon"', which depicts the Man sliding down to the earth on a spidery thread; see our *J.R.R. Tolkien: Artist and Illustrator* (1995), fig. 45.

Both poem and picture in turn are related to the appearance of the moon in the early 'Silmarillion' text *The Book of Lost Tales* (*c.* 1916–20): an island of glass, crystal, or silver, with a white turret from which an aged Elf, a stowaway on 'the Ship of the Moon', 'watches the heavens, or the world beneath, and that is Uolë Kúvion who sleepeth never. Some indeed have named him the Man in the Moon . . .' (*The Book of Lost Tales, Part One*, p. 193). Christopher Tolkien has commented that Uolë Kúvion 'seems almost to have strayed in from another conception', and that he was earlier called Uolë Mikúmi 'King of the Moon' (*The Book of Lost Tales, Part One*, p. 202). A 'pallid minaret / Dizzy and white at its lunar height' also appears, with yet another version of the Man in the Moon, in Tolkien's children's story *Roverandom* (conceived as an oral tale in 1925): 'It was white with pink and pale green lines in it, shimmering as if the tower were built of millions of seashells still wet with foam and gleaming; and the tower stood on the edge of a white precipice, white as a cliff of chalk, but shining with moonlight more brightly than a pane of glass far away on a cloudless night' (*Roverandom* (1998), p. 22).

Thomas Honegger has noted parallels between *The Man in the Moon Came Down Too Soon* and a much longer poem published in 1839–40, *The Man in the Moon*, by an unnamed undergraduate at Worcester College, Oxford. In this, the Man having become bored 'Of living so long in the land of dreams; / 'Twas a beautiful sphere, but nevertheless, / Its lunar life was passionless', he descends to earth like a falling star and seeks the 'woes / And joys of human life'. But the earlier poet quickly departs from the Man in the Moon of nursery tradition, transforming the character into a winged angel or sprite; and despite his shared Oxford connection, there is no evidence that Tolkien knew of the earlier work, nor any reason why he should have drawn upon it for his own. It does seem likely, though, that Tolkien knew *At the Back of the North Wind* (1870) by George MacDonald, in which the nursery rhyme 'Hey Diddle Diddle' is combined with the traditional 'Man in the Moon' verse quoted above (see also our notes for *The Man in the Moon Stayed Up Too Late*):

> But the man in the moon,
>   Coming back too soon
> From the famous town of Norwich,
>   Caught up the dish,
>   Said, 'It's just what I wish
> To hold my cold plum-porridge!'

Gave the cow a rat-tat,
Flung water on the cat,
And sent him away like a rocket.
Said, 'O Moon there you are!'
Got into her car,
And went off with the spoon in his pocket.

Hey ho! diddle, diddle!
The wet cat and wet fiddle,
They made such a caterwauling,
That the cow in a fright
Stood bolt upright
Bellowing now, and bawling;
And the dog on his tail,
Stretched his neck with a wail.
But 'Ho! ho!' said the man in the moon —
'No more in the South
Shall I burn my mouth,
For I've found a dish and a spoon.'

In revising and enlarging *Why the Man in the Moon Came Down Too Soon* for the *Bombadil* collection, Tolkien introduced references to Middle-earth geography while eliminating those to Norwich and England. The 1962 version is said in the *Bombadil* preface to be one of two poems (with *The Last Ship*) 'derived ultimately from Gondor. [These] are evidently based on the traditions of Men, living in shorelands and familiar with rivers running into the Sea. No. 6 [the present poem] actually mentions *Belfalas* (the windy bay of Bel [the Bay of Belfalas, south of the kingdom of Gondor]) and the Sea-ward Tower, *Tirith Aear*, of Dol Amroth [the chief city and port of Belfalas]. . . .' Among other differences, the Man is crowned with opals rather than gold, and pearls adorn his *girdlestead* (waist). Instead of a 'silken robe', he wears a '*mantle* grey' (a grey cloak, but no longer a 'faerie cloak'). His tower is made of *moonstone* (the literal meaning of *selenite*), and he is taken to land by 'a fisherman's boat' (no longer a 'Yarmouth boat'), now against his wish rather than because of it. Only a single tower, not fifty, tells the news of his '*moonsick* cruise': here Tolkien chose an old word with the same meaning as the one he used in the earlier poem, *lunatic*, and moved the latter to the end of the revised poem, where the Man's quest is 'lunatic' rather than 'adventurous'. *Lunatic* is highly appropriate to the context of the poem, with its element *luna-* (Latin 'moon'), reflecting a belief that changes of the moon cause insanity.

In the revision, despite 'hunger or *drouth*' (drought, or rather, thirst) the Man receives no refreshment, indeed less than before, until he pays an even higher price than in the earlier poem. The punch and the 'peppery stew' he desires in the 1923 version became in 1962 'pepper [for meat], and punch galore', with punch and 'peppery *brew*' in the intervening text (*The Book of Lost Tales, Part One*, p. 205). The time of the Man's visit to earth also changed, becoming 'ere Yule': in the context of Middle-earth, this is a period of winter holidays, but the reader is meant to think of Christmas, when 'puddings of Yule with plums' are traditionally served. The Man in the Moon has arrived 'so much too soon' for this dish, the 'plum-porridge' of the earlier version, that is, much too early in the year. *Plum* in 'plum-porridge' (or 'plum pudding') tends to refer to prunes, i.e. dried plums, or to any kind of dried fruit, such as currants, raisins, or sultanas. The plum-porridge (or plum-pottage) of old was very different from today's plum pudding, more liquid than firm, and savoury (with meat) rather than sweet.

In December 1927, Tolkien wrote a letter to his children in the guise of 'Father Christmas' (one of many such letters written between 1920 and 1943), in which the Man in the Moon visits the North Pole. 'The Man in the Moon paid me a visit the other day', Father Christmas relates; 'he often does about this time, as he gets lonely in the Moon, and we make him a nice little Plum Pudding (he is so fond of things with plums in!)' (*Letters from Father Christmas* (1999 edn.), p. 33). Given brandy by the North Polar Bear, the man falls fast asleep; and in his absence from the moon, dragons came out and obscure its light (evidently a reference to the lunar eclipse of 8 December that year). The Man awakes to set things right only just in time.

Although Tolkien judged Pauline Baynes's large illustration for *The Man in the Moon Came Down Too Soon* relatively in keeping with the 'world' of the *Bombadil* poems, he felt that it was 'defective as an illustration in making the Man's garment too like a nightgown and omitting crown, belt, and cloak' (letter to Rayner Unwin, 29 August 1962, A&U archive).

THE STONE TROLL

The earliest version of *The Stone Troll* was called *Pēro & Pōdex* (Latin 'Boot and Bottom'). Revised as *The Root of the Boot*, it was included with other poems by Tolkien and by a colleague at the University of Leeds, E.V. Gordon, together with selections from Icelandic student songbooks, assembled by Gordon in the first half of the 1920s to amuse and encourage students in the Leeds English school. In 1935 or 1936, A.H. Smith, formerly a student at Leeds, gave a copy of the 'Leeds Songs' to a group of students at University College, London to print on an historic press; and in this way, *The Root of the Boot* was published (with twelve other poems by Tolkien) in the booklet *Songs for the Philologists* (1936):

A troll sat alone on his seat of stone,
And munched and mumbled a bare old bone;

And long and long he had sat there lone
   And seen no man nor mortal —
      Ortal! Portal!
And long and long he had sat there lone
   And seen no man nor mortal.

Up came Tom with his big boots on;
'Hallo!' says he, 'pray what is yon?
It looks like the leg o' me nuncle John
   As should be a-lyin' in churchyard.
      Searchyard, Birchyard!' *etc.*

'Young man', says the troll, 'that bone I stole;
But what be bones, when mayhap the soul
In heaven on high hath an aureole
   As big and as bright as a bonfire?
      On fire, yon fire.'

Says Tom: 'Oddsteeth! 'tis my belief,
If bonfire there be, 'tis underneath;
For old man John was as proper a thief
   As ever wore black on a Sunday —
      Grundy, Monday!

But still I doan't see what is that to thee,
Wi' me kith and me kin a-makin' free:
So get to hell and ax leave o' he,
    Afore thou gnaws me nuncle!
      Uncle, Buncle!'

In the proper place upon the base
Tom boots him right — but, alas! that race
Hath a stonier seat than its stony face;
    So he rued that root on the rumpo,
      Lumpo, Bumpo!

Now Tom goes lame since home he came,
And his bootless foot is grievous game;
But troll's old seat is much the same,
    And the bone he boned from its owner!
      Donor, Boner!

As a point of comparison with *The Root of the Boot*, the sixth stanza in *Pēro & Pōdex* reads (*The Return of the Shadow*, p. 144):

In the proper place upon the base
Tom boots him right — but, alas! that race

> Hath as stony a seat as it is in face,
> And Pero was punished by Podex.
> Odex! Codex!

The complete manuscript of *Pēro & Pōdex* is transcribed in *The History of The Hobbit, Part One: Mr. Baggins* by John D. Rateliff (2007), pp. 101–2.

Tolkien made several corrections to *The Root of the Boot* in a personal copy of *Songs for the Philologists*, reflected in the text printed above (and see *The Return of the Shadow*, pp. 142–3). He also changed the third line of the third stanza from 'In heaven on high hath an *aureole*' (halo, celestial crown) to 'Hath a halo in heaven upon its *poll*' (the human head), and suggested that 'proper' in the penultimate verse might be 'prapper', a pronunciation more in keeping with Tom's dialectal English. In the second stanza, 'me nuncle' is Tom's version of 'my nuncle', that is, 'mine uncle', *mine* once having been used as a possessive pronoun, instead of *my*, when the following word (like *uncle*) began with a vowel. In the fifth stanza, 'ax leave' is a version of 'ask leave' (compare 'axin' leave' for 'asking leave' in *The Stone Troll*). Tom's speech is characterized by clipped speech (*a-lyin'*, *a-makin'*) and broad vowels (*doan't* for 'don't').

Here *Mumbled* means 'bite or chew with the gums, or without much use of teeth, or to fondle with the lips'. *Oddsteeth* is an abbreviation of the Elizabethan oath 'God's teeth'. John is not in heaven, Tom says, but 'underneath', in hell, for he was a thief, albeit one who piously wore black on Sunday; in any event, John is Tom's relation ('kith and kin'). In the final stanza, *boned* is a verb meaning 'stole', playing on *bone* as a noun (compare, in the third verse, 'that bone I stole'). The two words at the end of each stanza which rhyme with the final word of each fourth line – such as *ortal* and *portal*, as rhymes for *mortal* – generally have no meaning of note, except for 'Grundy, Monday' at the end of the fourth stanza, which refers to the nursery rhyme which begins 'Solomon Grundy, / born on a Monday'.

Tolkien noted in his copy of *Songs for the Philologists* that *The Root of the Boot* was to be sung to the tune of 'The Fox Went Out'. This English folk song begins:

The Fox went out on a chilly night
He prayed for the moon to give him light
For he had many a mile to go that night
Before he reached the town-o, town-o, town-o
He had many a mile to go that night
Before he reached the town-o

Christopher Tolkien has said that his father 'was extremely fond of this song, which went to the tune of *The fox went out on a winter's night* [the lyrics vary], and my delight in the line *If bonfire there be, 'tis underneath* is among my very early recollections' (*The Return of the Shadow*, p. 142).

When Tolkien needed a song for Bingo (later Frodo) to sing at the inn at Bree in Book I, Chapter 9 of *The Lord of the Rings*, his first choice was *The Root of the Boot*, but almost immediately he substituted *The Man in the Moon Stayed Up Too Late*. Eventually he used the 'troll song' for a comic turn by Sam Gamgee in Book I, Chapter 12, and that only after deciding that it should not be sung later in the story, in the house of Elrond (where, instead, Bilbo chants *Eärendil Was a Mariner*; see our notes for *Errantry*). The final version of Sam's song, as published in *The Lord of the Rings*, was reprinted in the *Bombadil* collection, with only one small change in punctuation, as *The Stone Troll*.

That text was reached, however, only after several revisions, one of which was printed and discussed by Christopher Tolkien in *The Treason of Isengard*, pp. 59–61. This draft version is notable for many alterations, especially the substitution of 'John' for 'Tom' and 'Jim' for 'Tim', the omission of references to Christian practice such as 'churchyard' and 'wore black on a Sunday', and a different outcome for the troll. Here, John having delivered his kick (breaking both boot and toe, but not the 'stony seat'), the troll 'tumbled down, and he cracked his crown', and

> There the troll lies, no more to rise,
> With his nose to earth and his seat to the skies;
> But under the stone is a bare old bone
> That was stole by a troll from its owner.
> Donor! Boner!
> Under the stone lies a broken bone
> That was stole by a troll from its owner.

Tolkien had a later draft of the poem in hand when he tape-recorded it in 1952 (see our introduction), and sang it to a tune different from the one commonly found in recordings of 'The Fox Went Out'.

In the final poem, the troll has 'gnawed [the bone] *near*' (closely and thoroughly). In the fourth stanza, one of the rhyming words, *trover*, is apt under the circumstances (Tom demanding that his uncle's shinbone be handed over), as this is a legal term which means 'compel the payment of damages by someone who has made improper use of one's property'. The troll's reply, that 'for a couple o' pins' he would eat Tom too, refers to *pin* as something of little or no value, as in the saying 'not worth a pin'. At this, Tom kicks the troll 'to *larn* him', that is, to '*learn* him', in the ancient sense of 'teach' (now archaic or slang); and as a result, his leg is *game* (lame).

Artist Pauline Baynes interpreted the name 'Tom' – associated, maybe, with the character's 'big boots' – to refer to Tom Bombadil, and drew him accordingly in one of her illustrations for *The Stone Troll*. The history of the work makes it clear, however, that Tolkien did not intend 'Tom' (or 'John') to be any character in particular, and in the context of *The Lord of the Rings*, as Sam says (bk. I, ch. 12), the poem is 'just a bit of nonsense'.

PERRY-THE-WINKLE

Perry-the-Winkle is a revision of a poem originally enti-
tled *The Bumpus*, one of a series of works Tolkien wrote
c. 1928, the 'Tales and Songs of Bimble Bay', centred
on an imaginary English coastal town and harbour.
Six poems in this series are known, and of these, three
so far have been published: *The Dragon's Visit*, *Glip*,
and *Progress in Bimble Town* (all are most conveniently
found in the second edition (2002) of *The Annotated
Hobbit*, edited by Douglas A. Anderson). Christopher
Tolkien kindly sent us three versions of *The Bumpus* for
comparison with *Perry-the-Winkle*, which has no earlier
published text. Following is the second (manuscript)
version, which closely follows the first but includes
several new features, notably mentions of Bimble Bay
(revised from 'the beautiful land of Bong') and of
'Mountains Blue', the Blue Mountains mentioned also
in *The Dragon's Visit*, 'where dragons live' (not to be
confused with the Ered Luin of Middle-earth):

The Bumpus sat on an old grey stone
    And sang his lonely lay:
'O why, O why should I live all alone
    In the hills of Bimble Bay?
The grass is green, the sky is blue,
    The sun shines on the sea,
But the Dragons have crossed the Mountains Blue
    And come no more to me.

No Trolls or Ogres are left at all,
    But People slam the door
Whenever they hear my flat feet fall
    Or my tail along the floor.'
He stroked his tail and looked at his feet,
    And he said: 'They may be long,
But my heart is kind, and my smile is sweet,
    And sweet and soft my song.'

The Bumpus went out, and who did he meet
    But old Mrs. Thomas and all
With umbrella and basket walking the street;
    And softly he did call:
'Dear Mrs. Thomas, good day to you?
    I hope you are quite well?'

But she dropped her brolly and basket too
   And yelled a frightful yell.

Policeman Pott was a-standing near;
   When he heard that awful cry,
He turned all purple and pink with fear,
   And swiftly turned to fly.
The Bumpus followed surprised and sad:
   'Don't go!' he gently said;
But old Mrs. Thomas ran home like mad,
   And hid beneath her bed.

The Bumpus then came to the market-place
   And looked up over the walls.
The sheep went wild when they saw his face;
   The cows jumped out of their stalls.
Old Farmer Hogg he spilled his beer;
   And the butcher threw his knives;
And Harry and his father howled with fear
   And ran to save their lives.

The Bumpus sadly sat and wept
   Outside the cottage door;
And William Winkle out he crept,

And sat down on the floor:
'Why do you weep, you great big lump,
    And wash the step like rain?'
The Bumpus gave his tail a thump,
    And smiled a smile again.

'O William Winkle, my lad,' he said,
    'Come, you're the boy for me,
And though you ought to be in bed
    I'll take you home to tea.
Jump on my back, and hold on tight!'
    And off they went flop flap,
And William had a feast that night,
    And sat on the Bumpus' lap.

There was buttered toast, and pikelets too,
    And jam and cream and cake;
And the Bumpus made some scrumptious Gloo,
    And showed him how to bake —
To bake the beautiful Bumpus-bread,
    And bannocks light and brown;
And then he tucked him up in a bed
    Of feathers and thistle-down.

'Bill Winkle, where have you been?' they said.
   'I have been to a Bumpus-tea,
And I feel so fat, for I have fed
   On Bumpus-bread,' said he.
The People all knocked at the Bumpus' door:
   'A beautiful Bumpus-cake
O bake for us, please!' they all now roar,
   'O bake, O bake, O bake!'

Policeman Pott came puffing fast,
   And made them form a queue,
And old Mrs. Thomas was late and last,
   And her bonnet was all askew.
'Go home! go home!' the Bumpus said.
   'Too many there are of you!
Only on Thursdays I bake my bread,
   And only for one or two.

Go home! go home, for goodness sake!
   I did not expect a call.
I have no pikelets, toast or cake,
   For William has eaten all.
Old Mrs. Thomas and Mr. Pott
   I wish no more to see.

Good bye! Don't argue, it's much too hot —
    Bill Winkle's the boy for me!'

Now William Winkle, he grew so fat
    A-eating of Bumpus-bread,
His weskit bust, and never a hat
    Would sit upon his head.
But Every Thursday he went to Tea
    And sat on the kitchen mat;
And smaller the Bumpus seemed to be,
    As he grew fat and fat.

And Bill a Baker great became:
    From Bimble Bay to Bong,
From sea to sea there went the fame
    Of his bread both short and long.
But it war'nt so good as Bumpus-bread;
    No jam was like the Gloo
That Every Thursday the Bumpus spread,
    And William used to chew!

The third version, a typescript entitled *William and the Bumpus*, includes a few more lines concerning the Bumpus teaching William the baker's art, and in other respects begins to approach the poem of 1962 – here, for instance, the Bumpus complains that his 'cooking [is] good enough', though many further additions and changes were yet to be made.

The Bumpus is an outlandish creature. It has a tail long enough to 'thump', flat, flapping feet, and a lap in which William can sit. The words of the poem leave its form unclear; in the first manuscript, however, Tolkien drew a sketch of the Bumpus as a plump, smiling, lizard-like figure with an apron around its waist. Neither we nor Christopher Tolkien can say if *Bumpus* had any special significance to the author of the poem, except as the name of a well-known London bookseller of the day. In the transition to *Perry-the-Winkle*, the Bumpus became 'the lonely troll', but the place-name 'Bumpus Head' remained in *The Dragon's Visit*.

An investigation of the name *Winkle*, an existing surname, could exhaust many pages; but the most promising connection, suggested by the title of the revised poem, seems to be with the shortened form of *periwinkle*, in the sense of an edible mollusc rather than of the trailing plant *Vinca*. *Brolly* in the third stanza of *The Bumpus* is slang for 'umbrella'. *Bong* in the final stanza appears to have no more meaning than as a convenient, Edward Learian rhyme for 'long'.

A *pikelet* is a small round teacake, and a *bannock* a

round, flat loaf. We find no source for *cramsome*, and must suppose that it is a Tolkien coinage after the verb *cram* 'overfeed, stuff, fill to satiety' (*Oxford English Dictionary*) or the noun meaning 'a dough or paste used in fattening poultry' or more generally for any food used to fatten animals. In *Perry-the-Winkle* 'cramsome' replaced 'Bumpus-' as in 'Bumpus-bread', 'Bumpus-cake', while 'a Bumpus-tea' became 'a fulsome tea'. The ingredients of the Bumpus' or Troll's prized baked goods, let alone of the 'scrumptious Gloo', unfortunately remain a mystery.

Moke, by which some People journey to the old Troll's home in *Perry-the-Winkle*, is a dialect word for 'donkey'. *Weskit* is a variation on *waistcoat* (American *vest*).

In the editorial fiction of the *Bombadil* preface, Tolkien says that *Perry-the-Winkle* ('No. 8') is marked in the Red Book 'SG [Sam Gamgee], and the ascription may be accepted'. A typescript of the poem preserved in the Bodleian Library (MS Tolkien 19, f. 51) contains the heading 'a children's song in the Shire (attributed to Master Samwise)'. The main points of transition from *The Bumpus* to *Perry-the-Winkle*, besides the change to the kind of creature the 'Winkle' meets, involved placing the events of the poem firmly in Hobbit country rather than the region of Bimble Bay. Thus Tolkien included, as alterations to the earlier text or in added lines or stanzas, references to the *Shire*; to *Delving*, or Michel Delving, the chief township of the Shire, with its *Lockholes* or jail; to *Bree*, the settlement of Hobbits and Men east of the Shire; and to *Weathertop*, a hill north-east of Bree. *Faraway*, as in 'hills of Faraway', appears as a place-name nowhere else in the Middle-earth corpus; in *Perry-the-Winkle* the name replaces and achieves the same rhyme as 'Bimble Bay' in *The Bumpus*.

THE MEWLIPS

The precursor to *The Mewlips* was published in the *Oxford Magazine* for 18 February 1937, as *Knocking at the Door: Lines Induced by Sensations When Waiting for an Answer at the Door of an Exalted Academic Person*:

> The places where the Mewlips dwell
>   Are dark as deepest ink,
> And slow and softly rings the bell,
>   As in the bog you sink.
>
> You sink into the bog, who dare
>   To knock upon their door,
> While fireworks flicker in the air
>   And shine upon the shore.
>
> The sparks hiss on the floors of sand
>   All wet with weeping fountains,

Where grey the glooming gargoyles stand
    Beneath the Morlock Mountains.

Over the Morlock Mountains, a long and weary
        way,
    Down in mouldy valleys where trees are wet and
        grey,
By the dark pools' borders without wind or tide,
    Moonless and sunless, there the Mewlips hide.

The caverns where the Mewlips sit
    Are cool as cellars old
With single sickly candle lit;
    And wet the walls of gold.

Their walls are wet, their ceilings drip;
    Their feet upon the floor
Go splashing with a squish-flap-flip,
    As they sidle to the door.

They peep out slyly through a crack
    All cased like armadilloes,
And your bones they gather in a sack
    Beneath the weeping willows.

Beyond the Morlock Mountains, a long and lonely
　　road,
Through the spider-shadows and the marsh of
　　Toad,
And through the wood of hanging trees and the
　　gallows-weed,
You go to find the Mewlips — and the Mewlips
　　feed.

Tolkien seems to have written *Knocking at the Door* in 1927, and revised it for publication ten years later. It appeared in the *Oxford Magazine* under a pseudonym, 'Oxymore', as in *oxymoron*, a joining of contradictory ideas. Its subtitle did not appear in the initial manuscript, only in an early, heavily emended typescript (both kindly supplied to us by Christopher Tolkien), and there read 'Lines Induced by Sensations on Waiting for an Answer at the Door of a Reverend and Academic Person'. At some point, Tolkien struck this through, then restored it, as if he could not decide if the poem was to be seen (if its subtitle were taken at face value) as a satire on university life.

In the typescript, among many revisions, the reading 'Morlock mountains' (*sic*) superseded 'Mingol mountains', where *Mingol* may have had no meaning other than as a name to alliterate with 'mountains'. Later, *Morlock* became (the probably meaningless) *Merlock*, perhaps because the former is a name associated with *The Time Machine* by H.G. Wells (1895). The curiously incongruous reading 'cased like *armadilloes*', referring to the small mammal known for its bony armour plates, was also a change made in the typescript.

In a letter of 13 February 1963 to a Miss Allen, who had asked questions about *The Mewlips*, Tolkien explained (or perhaps invented at that moment) that Mewlips were merely legend to Hobbits, nor would Hobbit minds dwell only on comforts – implying, it seems, that from time to time they would turn to the macabre, to the likes of 'grinning *gargoyles*' (grotesque figures) and '*noisome* waters' (with an offensive smell), in the way that fairy-stories by the Grimms or Andrew Lang, unexpurgated, can be (or are thought by some to be) the stuff of nightmares. Tolkien does not explain the name *Mewlips*, nor can the landmarks mentioned in the 1962 poem – the Merlock Mountains, the marsh of Tode ('Toad' in 1937) – be located reliably in Middle-earth. 'Spider-shadows' recalls the forest of Mirkwood in *The Hobbit*, or the darkness surrounding Ungoliant in 'The Silmarillion', and a stand of 'drooping willows' beside a 'rotting river-strand' might be found in the

Old Forest in *The Lord of the Rings*; but such a connection should not be forced. *The Mewlips* in fact is the only poem in the *Bombadil* volume not mentioned by Tolkien in the preface, by number or allusion, not even among the 'marginalia' which include those works 'often unintelligible even when legible'. It was one of the last of the poems Tolkien drew from his papers, and one which he felt would need 'thorough re-handling' for the collection (letter to Rayner Unwin, 5 February 1962, A&U archive).

Gorcrow (*gore* + *crow*) is a name for the carrion-crow. We cannot find *gallows-weed* in any dictionary, but it may be that Tolkien meant it as a variation on *gallow-grass*, or hemp (used to make ropes for hanging by a gallows).

OLIPHAUNT

Oliphaunt was first published in Book IV, Chapter 3 of *The Lord of the Rings* (*The Two Towers*, 1954), where it is recited by Sam Gamgee. 'That's a rhyme we have in the Shire,' he explains. 'Nonsense maybe, and maybe not. But we have our tales too, and news out of the South, you know.' When Sam finally sees an 'oliphaunt' (elephant) in the flesh – the Mûmak of Harad, in Book IV, Chapter 4 – he finds it a far greater beast than the one in his poem: 'a grey-clad moving hill', the like of which 'does not walk now in Middle-earth', a mammoth or mastodon in all but name. The 'facts' Sam presents in his verse are found also in medieval bestiaries: the elephant's enormous size (like a mountain), the snake-like appearance of its trunk, its ivory tusks, its longevity, its capacity to smash and squash.

Alongside and informing the bestiaries was a much earlier text known as *Physiologus* ('Naturalist'). This lent its name, at least, as the 'source' of two poems that Tolkien published in the *Stapeldon Magazine* for June 1927, with the shared title 'Adventures in Unnatural History and Medieval Metres, Being the Freaks of Fisiologus': *Iumbo, or ye Kinde of ye Oliphaunt*, and *Fastitocalon* (see further below). (Two more 'bestiary' poems by Tolkien, like *Iumbo* and *Fastitocalon* written probably in the 1920s, remain unpublished: *Reginhardus, the Fox* and *Monoceros, the Unicorn*.) *Iumbo*, reprinted here, is divided in the bestiary manner, with the natural history of a creature (*natura*) followed by a Christian moral or spiritual meaning (*significacio*), but it departs almost at once from the medieval tradition into a modern world of flannel (cloth), rubber hoses, and vacuum cleaners.

Natura iumbonis.

The Indic oliphaunt's a burly lump,
A moving mountain, a majestic mammal
(But those that fancy that he wears a hump
Confuse him incorrectly with the camel).
His pendulous ears they flap about like flannel;
He trails a supple elongated nose
That twixt his tusks of pearly-white enamel
Performs the functions of a rubber hose
Or vacuum cleaner as his needs impose,

Or on occasion serves in trumpet's stead,
Whose fearful fanfares utterly surpass
In mighty music from his monstrous head
The hollow boom of bells or bands of brass.
Nor do these creatures quarrel (as alas!
Do neighbours musical in Western lands);
In congregations do they tramp the grass,
And munch the juicy shoots in friendly bands,
Till not a leaf unmasticated stands.

This social soul one unconvivial flaw
Has nonetheless: he's poor in repartee,
His jests are heavy, for Mohammed's law
He loves, and though he has the thirst of three,
His vast interior he fills with tea.
Not thus do water-drinkers vice escape,
And weighty authors state that privily
He takes a drug, more deadly than the grape,
Compared with which cocaine's a harmless jape.

The dark mandragora's unwholesome root
He chews with relish secret and unholy,
Despising other pharmaceutic loot
(As terebinth, athansie, or moly).
Those diabolic juices coursing slowly

Do fill his sluggish veins with sudden madness,
Changing his grave and simple nature wholly
To a lamb titanic capering in gladness,
A brobdingnagian basilisk in badness.

The vacuous spaces of his empty head
Are filled with fires of fell intoxication;
His legs endure no longer to be led,
But wander free in strange emancipation.
Then frightful fear amid his exaltation
Awakes within him lest he tumble flat,
For apparatus none for levitation
Has he, who falling down must feebly bat
The air with legs inadequate and fat.

Then does he haste, if he can coax his limbs,
To some deep silent water or dark pool
(Where no reptilian mugger lurks or swims)
And there he stands — no! not his brow to cool,
But thinking that he cannot fall, the fool,
Buoyed by his belly adipose and round.
Yet if he find no water, as a rule,
He blindly blunders thumping o'er the ground,
And villages invades with thunderous sound.

If any house oppose his brutish bump,
Then woe betide — it crumples in a heap,
Its inmates jumbled in a jellied lump
Pulped unexpecting in imprudent sleep.
When tired at last, as tame as any sheep
Or jaded nag, he longs for sweet repose,
In Ind a tree, whose roots like serpents creep,
Of girth gigantic opportunely grows,
Whereon to lean his weary bulk and doze.

Thus will his dreams not end in sudden jerk,
He thinks. What hopes! For hunters all too well
Acquainted with his little habits lurk
Beneath the Upus' shade; a nasty sell
For Oliphas they plan, his funeral knell.
With saws they wellnigh sever all the bole,
Then cunning prop it, that he may not tell,
Until thereto he trusts his weight, poor soul —
It all gives way and lands him in a hole.

Significacio.

The doctrine that these mournful facts propound
Needs scarcely pointing, yet we cannot blink
The fact that some still follow base Mahound,

Though Christian people universally think
That water neat is hardly fit to drink.
Not music nor fat feeding make a feast
But wine, and plenty of it. Good men wink
At fun and frolic (though too well policed)
When mildly canned or innocently greased;
But those whose frenzy's root is drugs not drink
Should promptly be suppressed and popped in
    clink.

The word *oliphaunt* is merely an archaic or 'rustic'
form of *elephant*, and a common medieval spelling. The
name *Iumbo* is 'Jumbo' in the classical Latin alphabet,
which did not have the letter J, and a nod to the famed
zoo and circus elephant Jumbo of the later nineteenth
century. That Jumbo, however, was an African ele-
phant, rather than the *Indic* ('Indian') variety featured
in the poem.

There appears to be no description in medieval
literature of the elephant abstaining from alcohol
('Mohammed's law', a prohibition in Islam) or drink-
ing tea. But the elephant is said by the bestiary authors
to be so inherently chaste that when it wants to con-
ceive, it must eat *mandragora*, or mandrake, a reputed
fertility drug and aphrodisiac, compared by Tolkien

to cocaine (in degree 'a harmless *jape*' or joke) and to three more benign items from the medieval phar-macopeia: *terebinth*, a tree which yields turpentine; *athanasie*, or tansy; and *moly* or 'sorcerer's garlic', the herb given by Hermes to Odysseus as a charm against Circe. Under the 'diabolic' influence of mandrake, taken *privily* (privately) and 'more dangerous than the grape' (wine), the elephant's 'grave and simple nature' becomes that of the *basilisk*, the most terrible of all bestiary creatures, with a lethal gaze or breath. Moreover, the elephant's 'badness' is then *brobding-nagian* in degree (after Brobdingnag, a land in Swift's *Gulliver's Travels* (1726) where everything is enormous relative to Gulliver).

According to the bestiaries, the elephant lives in fear of falling down – its legs were thought to have no joints – and to prevent this, he often stands in water, where he is 'buoyed by his belly adipose [fat] and round'. 'Where no reptilian mugger lurks or swims' presumably refers to the *mugger* or broad-nosed crocodile of India. In the bestiaries, a traditional enemy of the elephant is said to be the dragon, but (it seems relevant to note) in 'The Elephant's Child', one of the *Just So Stories* by Rudyard Kipling (1902), the elephant gains its long nose through an encounter with a crocodile.

The bestiaries note as well that because the elephant (they say) has a habit of sleeping while leaning against a tree, hunters would set a trap by cutting a favoured tree in half, so that it would collapse under the elephant's weight and leave the creature defenceless, unable to rise. The 'tree, whose roots like serpents creep' is the *Upas*, which appears in travellers' tales, and most notably in Erasmus Darwin's *Botanic Garden* (1789–91):

Fierce in dread silence on the blasted heath,
Fell Upas sits, the Hydra tree of death.
Lo from one root the envenomed soil below,
A thousand vegetable serpents grow.

The Upas is indeed a large tree, but in height rather than 'girth gigantic', native to *Ind* (here Asia or the East), most famously Java; and for an elephant-hunter to cut into one, risking contact with its poisonous sap, would be dangerous indeed.

Tolkien's satire of the *Physiologus* concludes not with a moral lesson but with moral conflict, between drugs and drink. The exaggerated, tongue-in-cheek picture of 'wine, and plenty of it', the notion of Christians 'universally' embracing excess (in a nation traditionally of tea-drinkers), and the pursuit of 'fun and frolic' while *canned* or *greased* (intoxicated) are contrasted with Muslim abstinence. *Mahound* (or *Mahoun*) is a corrupt form of *Muhammad* (*Mohammed*, etc.), recorded from medieval times.

For *Oliphaunt* in *The Lord of the Rings*, Tolkien transformed *Iumbo* into a 'hobbit nursery-rhyme', as he wrote to his son Christopher in 1944 (*Letters*, p. 77). In the process, he made it much simpler and cleansed it of anachronisms not to be found in Middle-earth, though it still retains the flavour of its bestiary ancestors.

FASTITOCALON

Tolkien published an earlier poem entitled *Fastitocalon* in the *Stapeldon Magazine* for June 1927:

Natura fastitocalonis.

Old Fastitocalon is fat:
His grease the most stupendous vat,
   If He perchance were boiled,
Or tank or reservoir would fill,
Or make of margarine a hill,
   Or keep the wheels well oiled
      that squeak
On all the carts beneath the sun,
Or brew emulsion in a tun
   For those whose chests are weak!

He wallows on a bed of slime
In the Ocean's deep and weedy clime;

As merry organs roll,
So snores He solemn sweet and loud,
And thither tumble in a crowd
   The sardine, and the sole
       so flat,
And all the little foolish fry
Who pry about with goggle eye,
   The skipper and the sprat
       in glee
Approach the portals of His jaws;
What feast or frolic be the cause
   They enter in to see.

Alas! they come not ever thence;
The joke is all at their expense,
   As is the dinner too.
Yet are there times of storm and strife,
When equinoctial gales are rife,
   And there is much ado
       down there.
He finds the depths devoid of rest,
Then up He comes and on His chest
   Floats in the upper air.

His ribs are tender, and his eye
Is small and wicked, wondrous sly;
    His heart is black and fickle.
Beware his vast and blubbery back;
His slumbrous sides do not attack,
    Nor ever seek to tickle.
        Beware!
His dreams are not profound or deep,
He only plays at being asleep;
    His snoring is a snare.

He, floating on the inky sea,
A sunny island seems to be,
    Although a trifle bare.
Conniving gulls there strut and prink,
Their job it is to tip the wink,
    If any one lands there
        with kettle
To make a picnic tea, or get
Relief from sickness or the wet,
    Or some, perhaps, to settle.

Ah! foolish folk, who land on HIM,
And patent stoves proceed to trim,
    Or make incautious fires

To dry your clothes or warm a limb,
Who dance or prance about the glim —
 'Tis just what He desires.
    He grins.
And when He feels the heat He dives
Down to the deeps: you lose your lives
 Cut off amid your sins.

Significacio sequitur.

This mighty monster teaches us
That trespassing is dangerous,
 And perils lurk in wait
For curious folk who peep in doors
Of other folk, or dance on floors
 Too early or too late
    with jazz;
That too much grease is worse than none,
To spare the margarine on bun
 Content with what one has
    on hand;
That many noises loud and strong
Are neither music nor a song
 But only just a band.

Fastitocalon in this version, written probably not long before its publication, was one of two 'Adventures in Unnatural History and Medieval Metres, Being the Freaks of Fisiologus', modelled on accounts collected in medieval bestiaries and based in part on the earlier *Physiologus* ('Naturalist'; see our notes for *Iumbo* under *Oliphaunt*, above). Here again, a description of an animal's nature (*natura*) precedes a moral (*significacio sequitur*, 'meaning follows'); and once more, Tolkien introduces anachronisms, such as margarine and squeaky wheels, transforming a 'medieval' poem into a tale for our time.

On 5 March 1964, Tolkien wrote to Eileen Elgar about his *Bombadil* poem *Fastitocalon* (but his comments apply also, and first, to the *Stapeldon Magazine* version) that it is

a reduced and rewritten form, to suit hobbit fancy, of an item in old 'bestiaries'. I think it was remarkable that you perceived the Greekness of the name through its corruptions. This I took in fact from a fragment of an Anglo-Saxon bestiary that has survived [perhaps the tenth-century Exeter Book], thinking that it sounded comic and absurd enough to serve as a hobbit alteration of something more learned and elvish. . . . The learned name in this case seems to have been *Aspido-chelōne* 'turtle with a round shield (of hide)'. Of that *astitocalon* is a corruption no worse than many of the time; but I am afraid the F was put on by the versifier simply to make the name alliterate, as was compulsory for poets in his day, with the other words in his line. Shocking, or charming freedom, according to taste.

He says: *þam is noma cenned | fyrnstreama geflotan Fastitocalon*, 'to him is a name appointed, to the floater in the ancient tides, Fastitocalon'. The notion of the treacherous island that is really a monster seems to derive from the East: the marine turtles enlarged by myth-making fancy; and I left it at that. But in Europe the monster becomes mixed up with whales, and already in the Anglo-Saxon version he is given whale characteristics, such as feeding by trawling with an open mouth. In moralized bestiaries he is, of course, an allegory of the devil, and is so used by Milton. [*Letters*, pp. 343–4]

In the earlier *Fastitocalon*, the creature is explicitly a whale, whose *blubber* (fat) was once avidly sought for making oil. A *tun* is a brewer's vat, and rubbing *emulsion* (oil) on the chest is a common remedy. A *skipper* is a sea-pike, and a *sprat* a kind of herring; these, with the sardine and the sole (as Tolkien plays with alliteration), are attracted to the whale, here by the sweet sound of his snoring, like 'merry organs'; in the bestiary tradition, the whale attracts fishes by his breath, said to be as sweet as flowers.

When, at the equinoxes, stormy winds ('*equinoctial gales*') stir up the bottom of the sea, the whale, its back covered with sea-sand or shingle, rises to the surface, where it may be mistaken for an island – a deliberate ruse, while only pretending to sleep. The notion that sailors might land upon a whale, thinking it to be land, only to perish when it dives after feeling the heat of a fire, is from the bestiaries, and figures also in the medieval *Voyage of St Brendan*. In the poem, 'conniving gulls' are brought into service to *tip the wink*, or warn the whale when men arrive and *trim* (prepare) their *patent* (commercially manufactured) *stoves*. *Glim* here means 'a faint light', perhaps from a candle or lantern (cf. *glimmer, gleam*).

As the whale attracts fish and drags them down into the deep, say the bestiaries, so Satan attracts men weak in their faith and carries them to hell. In contrast, Tolkien's 'moral' condemns 'curious folk who peep in doors / Of other folk, or dance on floors . . . with jazz'.

It is in the vein of a comment he made years later to his son Christopher: '[postwar] music will give place to jiving: which as far as I can make out means holding a "jam session" round a piano (an instrument properly intended to produce the sounds devised by, say, Chopin) and hitting it so hard that it breaks' (31 July 1944, *Letters*, p. 89).

When he came to revise *Fastitocalon* for the *Bombadil* collection, Tolkien shortened and simplified, but retained the central idea of a false island, with birds deceptively sitting upon it, and a crafty beast – now properly (from *Aspido-chelōne*) a giant 'Turtle-fish' with a horny shell. 'Middle-earth' is mentioned almost at the end, to place the poem within the context of *The Lord of the Rings*, and its new 'moral' ('Set foot on no uncharted shore!') better suits an unadventurous Hobbit author.

In the first printing of the *Bombadil* volume, *Cat* (see below) preceded *Fastitocalon*, but because all two-colour art for the book had to be placed (as an economy measure) on only one side of the large sheet later folded to make a gathering, the full-page illustration for *Cat* was placed within the text of *Fastitocalon*. This was corrected, at publisher Rayner Unwin's advice and with Tolkien's agreement, in the second printing, where

Fastitocalon now preceded *Cat*. Thus the poems origi-
nally numbered 12 and 11 became 11 and 12; but the
references to 11 and 12 were not emended in Tolkien's
preface, where *Cat* (not *Fastitocalon*) was meant to be
included among the 'marginalia' in the Red Book, and
Fastitocalon (not *Cat*) was described as by Sam Gamgee
and a touched-up 'older piece of the comic bestiary
lore of which Hobbits appear to have been fond'.

CAT

Tolkien wrote *Cat* in 1956 for his granddaughter Joanna (Joan Anne), daughter of his second son, Michael. The poem was published for the first time in *The Adventures of Tom Bombadil and Other Verses from the Red Book*. For the re-ordering of *Cat* in the sequence of poems after the first printing, see our notes for *Fastitocalon*, above.

Tolkien commented to Rayner Unwin that although he found Pauline Baynes's large picture for *Cat* one of her best for the book, 'as an illustration, it misses a main point in not making one of the "thought-lions" engaged in *man*-eating' (29 August 1962, A&U archive; *Chronology*, p. 596). The poem refers to cats which 'in the East feasted on beasts and tender men'.

In medieval lore, a *pard* was a distinct species among the great cats, parti-coloured and with a lion's mane. Its attributes of speed and deadly violence – 'fleet upon feet', 'leaps on his meat' – are described in well-known bestiary manuscripts ('Pardus id est genus varium ac velocissimum et praeceps ad sanguinem, saltu enim ad mortem ruit'). It is said that the offspring of a lion (*leo*) and a pard is a leopard; but the zoological name for the leopard is *Panthera pardus*, and *pard* came to be used in a poetic or literary sense for 'leopard' or 'panther'.

SHADOW-BRIDE

An earlier version of *Shadow-Bride* was published in 1936 as *The Shadow Man*, in the twelfth *Annual* of Our Lady's School in Abingdon-on-Thames, near Oxford. Our Lady's School (now Our Lady's Abingdon) was founded in 1860 as a convent school by the Sisters of Mercy, a Roman Catholic order of nuns with whom Tolkien, himself a devout Catholic, was familiar since his days in hospital during the First World War.

> There was a man who dwelt alone
>   beneath the moon in shadow.
> He sat as long as lasting stone,
>   and yet he had no shadow.
> The owls, they perched upon his head
>   beneath the moon of summer;
> They wiped their beaks and thought him dead,
>   who sat there dumb all summer.

There came a lady clad in grey
   beneath the moon a-shining.
One moment did she stand and stay
   her hair with flowers entwining.
He woke, as had he sprung of stone,
   beneath the moon in shadow,
And clasped her fast, both flesh and bone;
   and they were clad in shadow.

And never more she walked in light,
   or over moonlit mountain,
But dwelt within the hill, where night
   is lit but with a fountain —
Save once a year when caverns yawn,
   and hills are clad in shadow,
They dance together then till dawn
   and cast a single shadow.

Almost the same text as that published in 1936 is preserved among Tolkien's papers in a fair copy manuscript, but with the title *Shadow-Bride*. Douglas A. Anderson in *The Annotated Hobbit* (2002 edn.) describes another manuscript version of *Shadow-Bride*, without a title and written on the same page as the poem *Elvish Song in Rivendell*; both appear to date from the early 1930s.

One possible analogue, first noted by Paul H. Kocher for *Shadow-Bride* but suited also to its precursor, is the myth of Persephone (Proserpine). In this, Hades (Pluto), ruler of the Underworld, abducts the maiden Persephone and takes her beneath the earth to be his wife. Her mother, Demeter (Ceres), goddess of the harvest, is so stricken with grief that the earth itself becomes desolate. At last, a bargain is struck, whereby (in some versions of the tale) Persephone returns to her mother each spring, but lives in the dark Underworld during winter, thus explaining the cycle of the seasons. If *The Shadow Man* and *Shadow-Bride* were inspired by this myth, the 'man who dwelt alone' is akin to Hades, master of darkness and shadow, and the 'lady clad in grey', entwining flowers in her hair, whom the man 'clasps fast' is Hades' bride, Persephone. In *The Shadow Man*, the man and lady dwell within a hill, a common expression of the Underworld (or Otherworld) in Celtic mythology; in *Shadow-Bride* this is 'below where neither days / nor any nights there are', a good description of the darkness of Hades' realm. The reference in both poems to 'once a year when caverns yawn', and especially in *Shadow-Bride* to the time when 'hidden things awake' – the return of spring after the long winter, or of growth after a drought – reinforces the comparison.

And yet, as Kocher comments, 'since discrepancies between [*Shadow-Bride*] and the legend are as numerous as the likenesses, dogmatism would be unwise' (*Master of Middle-earth: The Fiction of J.R.R. Tolkien* (1972), pp. 220–1). Hades is not said to have 'sat as long [or as still] as lasting [or carven] stone' before capturing Persephone (which he does by violent action), nor do both king and queen of the Underworld 'dance together then till dawn' at the appointed time of year. At the same time, neither poem is likely to be a treatment of sudden and binding love, given the strangeness of their imagery and events: this is not, for example, the 'Silmarillion' story of Beren coming upon Lúthien Tinúviel dancing among hemlocks, or of Thingol caught by the spell of Melian in the shadows of the trees.

Was the man of the poem lying in wait, or was he, before he woke, bound by a spell as explicitly in *Shadow-Bride*? Does he acquire a shadow when he wakes, as in *The Shadow Man*, or does he take and share the lady's, as in the revision? Is the lady an elf, as some critics have called her? In the latter case, it may be worth noting the poem *Ides Ælfscýne*, written by Tolkien in Old English in the 1920s, privately published in 1936 in *Songs for the Philologists*, and reprinted by Tom Shippey, with a translation, in *The Road to Middle-earth*: in this, a boy is embraced by an 'elf-fair lady' (*ides ælfscýne*), who takes him with her 'under the gloom, where the shadow-way always flickered' (2005 edn., p. 405).

For *The Shadow Man*, we are unable to explain the phrase 'where night / is lit but with a fountain' except perhaps as a reference to God in Psalm 36:9: 'For with thee is the fountain of life; in thy light shall we see light.'

THE HOARD

The Hoard is the last in a sequence of poems which began with *Iúmonna Gold Galdre Bewunden*, written possibly at the end of 1922 and published in the Leeds journal *The Gryphon* for January 1923. Tolkien revised *Iúmonna Gold Galdre Bewunden* extensively and published the second version under the same title (as printed, lacking the acute accent) in the *Oxford Magazine* for 4 March 1937; and this, in turn, became *The Hoard* in 1962, for the *Bombadil* collection, with a few further, minor alterations. 'The Hoard' as a title for the poem, however, existed by September 1946, when Tolkien used it to refer to a copy of the text – in whatever version was the latest by then – which he sent to George Allen & Unwin for possible publication with his story *Farmer Giles of Ham*. Here we reprint the first of the sequence, from *The Gryphon* (with one typographical error, 'His' for 'He', corrected in the third stanza):

There were elves olden and strong spells
Under green hills in hollow dells
They sang o'er the gold they wrought with mirth,
In the deeps of time in the young earth,
Ere Hell was digged, ere the dragons' brood
Or the dwarves were spawned in dungeons rude;
And men there were in a few lands
That caught some cunning of their mouths and
    hands.
Yet their doom came and their songs failed,
And greed that made them not to its holes haled
Their gems and gold and their loveliness,
And the shadows fell on Elfinesse.

There was an old dwarf in a deep grot
That counted the gold things he had got,
That the dwarves had stolen from men and elves
And kept in the dark to their gloomy selves.
His eyes grew dim and his ears dull,
And the skin was yellow on his old skull;
There ran unseen through his bony claw
The faint glimmer of gems without a flaw.
He heard not feet that shook the earth,
Nor the rush of wings, not the brazen mirth
Of dragons young in their fiery lust;

His hope was in gold and in jewels his trust.
Yet a dragon found his dark cold hole,
And he lost the earth and the things he stole.

There was an old dragon under an old stone
Blinking with red eyes all alone.
The flames of his fiery heart burnt dim;
He was knobbed and wrinkled and bent of limb;
His joy was dead and his cruel youth,
But his lust still smouldered and he had no ruth.
To the slime of his belly the gems stuck thick
And his things of gold he would snuff and lick
As he lay thereon and dreamed of the woe
And grinding anguish thieves should know
That ever set finger on one small ring;
And dreaming uneasy he stirred a wing.
He heard not the step nor the harness clink
Till the fearless warrior at his cavern's brink
Called him come out and fight for his gold,
Yet iron rent his heart with anguish cold.

There was an old king on a high throne;
His white beard was laid on his knees of bone,
And his mouth savoured nor meat nor drink,

Nor his ears song, he could only think
Of his huge chest with carven lid
Where the gold and jewels unseen lay hid
In a secret treasury in the dark ground,
Whose mighty doors were iron-bound.
The swords of his warriors did dull and rust,
His glory was tarnished and his rule unjust,
His halls hollow and his bowers cold,
But he was king of elfin gold.
He heard not the horns in the mountain pass,
He smelt not the blood on the trodden grass,
Yet his halls were burned and his kingdom lost,
In a grave unhonoured his bones were tossed.

There is an old hoard in a dark rock
Forgotten behind doors none can unlock.
The keys are lost and the path gone,
The mound unheeded that the grass grows on;
The sheep crop it and the larks rise
From its green mantle, and no man's eyes
Shall find its secret, till those return
Who wrought the treasure, till again burn
The lights of Faery, and the woods shake,
And songs long silent once more awake.

'Iúmonna gold galdre bewunden' is line 3052 of the Old English poem *Beowulf*, a work with which Tolkien as a scholar was closely concerned. The words mean, in his own translation (included in a letter to Pauline Baynes, 6 December 1961, *Letters*, p. 312), 'the gold of men of long ago enmeshed in enchantment', and refer in *Beowulf* to a great hoard gathered in ancient days, around which has been wound a spell or curse against any who would disturb it. The title is apt for Tolkien's poem, which explores through a series of episodes the 'curse' of greed and possessiveness.

All versions of the poem begin long ago, with elves singing as they work 'under green hills', making 'many fair things' (1937, 1962) with 'gems and gold' (1923). But greed brings (unnamed) foes to their wealth, and the elves are overthrown. Later, the treasure is held by 'an old dwarf in a deep *grot*' (cave), in the 1923 poem gained explicitly by theft: the dwarves have stolen 'gold things' and glimmering gems 'from men and elves'. In the revision, the dwarf is no longer named as a thief, yet has come to have 'silver and gold [to which] his fingers *clave*' (cleaved, stuck fast); and he is said himself to make precious things, not (like the Elves) for their beauty, but 'to buy the power of kings'. In the 1923 poem, his reclusion is only implied; in the later versions, it is made clear that when the dragon comes, he dies 'alone in the red fire' (1937, 1962).

The dragon of the third stanza, in turn, grows old and weak upon his hoard, while thinking ruthlessly ('he had no *ruth*', 1923), and to distraction, of what he would do to thieves. Figuratively chained to his treasure, like the old dwarf he cannot hold that for which 'his lust still smouldered' (1923). This, too, is the fate of the 'old king', obsessed with the wealth in 'his huge chest with carven lid', protecting it behind strong doors while fatally neglecting his kingdom. The swords of his warriors (*thanes* in 1937, 1962: in Anglo-Saxon England, men granted land in exchange for military service) are dull and rusted, if any remain to defend the king's 'hollow' halls and cold *bowers* (dwellings).

The irony of this final episode, as Tom Shippey has remarked, is that the hoard lay 'in secret treasury in the dark ground', and when the old king dies it is forgotten 'behind doors none can unlock' (1937, 1962). In the first *Iúmonna Gold Galdre Bewunden* the hoard lies 'unheeded' beneath a green mound, 'and no man's eyes / Shall find its secret, till those return / Who wrought the treasure'. The 1923 poem looks ahead to that time as a return to golden days, 'till again burn / The lights of Faery', while the later versions foretell indefinite loss,

'While gods wait and the elves sleep, / its old secret shall the earth keep' (1937), amended to 'The old hoard the Night shall keep, / while earth waits and the Elves sleep' (1962).

The dragon of the poems, to whose belly 'gems stuck thick', and who in the 1937 and 1962 versions 'knew the place of the least ring / beneath the shadow of his black wing', is a close cousin to Smaug in *The Hobbit* (first published 1937), with his 'waistcoat of fine diamonds', as well as kin to the *Beowulf* dragon, which sat upon its hoard for three hundred years. In Chapter 12 of *The Hobbit*, Bilbo enters Smaug's lair and steals a cup; Smaug soon misses it, though it is only the smallest part of a vast treasure. 'Dragons', Tolkien explains, 'may not have much real use for all their wealth, but they know it to an ounce as a rule, especially after long possession; and Smaug was no exception.' The dragon of the poems is also recalled in *The Hobbit* in Smaug's 'uneasy dream', 'in which a warrior, altogether insignificant in size but provided with a bitter sword and great courage, figured most unpleasantly'.

In the *Bombadil* preface, Tolkien writes of *The Hoard*, now imagined to have been written in the hobbits' Red Book, that it depended 'on the lore of Rivendell, Elvish and Númenórean, concerning the heroic days at the end of the First Age [of Middle-earth]; it seems to contain echoes of the Númenórean tale of Túrin and Mîm the Dwarf'. *Rivendell*, in *The Hobbit* and *The Lord of the Rings*, is an Elvish stronghold, and in the Prologue to *The Lord of the Rings* is said to have been an important source of information for Hobbit historians. *Númenor* was an island kingdom of Men, founded after the fall of the dark lord, Morgoth; at the end of the Second Age, Númenóreans came to Middle-earth and founded the realms of Arnor and Gondor. *Túrin* (Túrin Turambar), a Man, was one of the greatest warriors of the First Age; in 'The Silmarillion' (as it developed in the 1950s) he spares the life of Mîm the Petty-Dwarf. Mîm also figures in the mythology from its earlier tales, in connection with a dragon's hoard in the fortress of Nargothrond (though not at that time with Túrin): in the *Quenta Noldorinwa* (*c.* 1930), Mîm 'sat there in joy fingering the gold and gems, and letting them run ever through his hands; and he bound them to himself with many spells' (*The Shaping of Middle-earth* (1986), p. 132). Tolkien's reference to Mîm in the *Bombadil* preface was the first published mention of a character whose story would not be told in any form until *The Silmarillion* appeared in 1977, fifteen years later.

A connection between *The Hoard* and 'The Silmarillion' was also pursued by Tolkien in a letter to Mrs Eileen Elgar, 5 March 1964, in which he discussed the poem almost as if it were an epitome of the mythology. He explained that the 'gods' of the first stanza are demiurgic powers (the Ainur) who aided Ilúvatar (God) in singing the world into being, including silver and gold among all matter; and that although Dwarves were not allied to evil, they were naturally disposed to pass from the love of making things to a fierce possessiveness. One therefore could look at *The Hoard* (and its 1937 precursor only) for other elements of the mythology, such as *Elvenhome*, a name which typically refers to Eldamar, the home of the Elves in the distant West of Tolkien's fictional world, but in this context must mean, more broadly, the lands in which the elves live, or the Elvish people themselves. (In particular, one may think of the Elven realm of Doriath, and of its downfall: see *The Silmarillion*, ch. 22.) *Hell*, meanwhile, could refer, as it does in drafts of the mythology, to the dungeon-fortress of Angband. And in the poem as in 'The Silmarillion', Elves are created first among peoples, 'ere dwarf was bred'.

And yet, in 'The Silmarillion' as it stood in 1937 but not in the *Oxford Magazine* poem of that year (carried forward in 1962), the main labours of the Ainur took place long *before* the creation of the moon and sun; and it also must be said that 'When the moon was new and the sun young' is very much of a kind with 'once upon a time, long ago' as a traditional way to begin a story, whether or not it refers to an earlier conception. The *Iúmonna Gold Galdre Bewunden* of 1923, though with no reference to 'gods', also includes 'Silmarillion' echoes, for instance that the Elves sang under green hills (in *Elfinesse,* an earlier equivalent of *Elvenhome*) before 'dwarves were spawned in dungeons *rude*' (primitive). It is conceivable that the mythology – always a 'dominant construction' in Tolkien's thoughts (*Letters,* p. 346) – had an influence on the earlier poem's composition; but it need not have done. Literary treatments of hoards were abundant before 1923, if any were needed for inspiration, and the subjects of greed and power run like a thread through Tolkien's fiction, most significantly in *The Hobbit* with its 'dragon-sickness', *The Lord of the Rings* with its overmastering Ring, and the story of Fëanor and the Silmarils in 'The Silmarillion'.

On 6 December 1961, Tolkien wrote to Pauline Baynes that *The Hoard* should not be treated in her illustrations as 'light-hearted', but rather as a tale of the woes of 'successive (nameless) inheritors' of a treasure and 'a tapestry of antiquity' in which 'individual pity' is not to be deeply engaged. In response to Baynes having chosen *The Hoard* as her favourite among the *Bombadil* poems, Tolkien said that he 'was most interested. . . . For it is the least fluid [of the poems], being written in [a] mode rather resembling the older English verse' – that is, in the Anglo-Saxon manner, with a *caesura* or pause between each half-line (*Letters*, p. 312).

Tolkien approved Baynes's pictures in the *Bombadil* collection except for her full-page illustration for *The Hoard*. In a letter to Rayner Unwin, he wrote that 'in spite of the excellent Worm [dragon] [the picture] fails badly on the young warrior. This is an archaic and heroic theme . . . , but the young person, without helm or shield, looks like a Tudor lackey with some elements of late mediaeval armour on his legs. I understand the pictorial difficulties; but of course no dragon, however decrepit would lie with his head away from the entrance' (29 August 1962, A&U archive; *Chronology*, p. 596). Despite Tolkien's misgivings, the illustration was published, and continued to be reprinted; Baynes, however, took his criticism to heart and revised the picture for the Tolkien collection *Poems and Stories* (1980; reproduced in our introduction to the present book), improving in addition to the 'young warrior' and the dragon her rendering of the treasure, which in the 1962 volume is indistinct.

The 1923 and 1937 versions of *Iúmonna Gold Galdre Bewunden* were reprinted in *Beowulf and the Critics* (2002, revised edn. 2011), with analysis and alternate readings by editor Michael D.C. Drout. Tolkien included the poem as a 'digression' in an Oxford discussion of *Beowulf* in the early 1930s. The lecture, *Beowulf and the Critics*, revised and without the poem, became Tolkien's 1936 British Academy lecture, *Beowulf: The Monsters and the Critics*.

THE SEA-BELL

The Sea-Bell is a revised and expanded version of the poem *Looney*, which Tolkien wrote probably in 1932 or 1933 and published in the *Oxford Magazine* for 18 January 1934:

'Where have you been; what have you seen
    Walking in rags down the street?'

'I come from a land, where cold was the strand,
    Where no men were me to greet.

I came on a boat empty afloat.
    I sat me thereon; swift did it swim;
Sail-less it fled, oar-less it sped;
    The stony beaches faded dim.

It bore me away, wetted with spray,
    Wrapped in the mist, to another land;

Stars were glimmering; the shore was shimmering,
   Moon on the foam, silver the sand.
I gathered me stones whiter than bones,
   Pearls and crystals and glittering shells;
I climbed into meadows fluttered with shadows,
   Culling there flowers with shivering bells,
Garnering leaves and grasses in sheaves.
   I clad me in raiment jewel-green,
My body enfolded in purple and gold;
   Stars were in my eyes, and the moonsheen.

There was many a song all the night long
   Down in the valley, many a thing
Running to and fro: hares white as snow,
   Voles out of holes, moths on the wing
With lantern eyes. In quiet surprise
   Badgers were staring out of dark doors.
There was dancing there, wings in the air,
   Feet going quick on the green floors.

There came a dark cloud. I shouted aloud;
   Answer was none, as onward I went.
In my ears dinned a hurrying wind;
   My hair was a-blowing, my back was bent.
I walked in a wood; silent it stood

And no leaf bore; bare were the boughs.
There did I sit wandering in wit;
   Owls went by to their hollow house.

I journeyed away for a year and a day —
   Shadows were on me, stones beneath —
Under the hills, over the hills,
   And the wind a-whistling through the heath.
Birds there were flying, ceaselessly crying;
   Voices I heard in the grey caves
Down by the shore. The water was frore,
   Mist was there lying on the long waves.

There stood the boat, still did it float
   In the tide spinning, on the water tossing.
I sat me therein; swift did it swim
   The waves climbing, the seas crossing,
Passing old hulls clustered with gulls,
   And the great ships laden with light,
Coming to haven, dark as a raven,
   Silent as owl, deep in the night.

Houses were shuttered, wind round them muttered;
   Roads were all empty. I sat by a door
In pattering rain, counting my gain:

Only withering leaves and pebbles I bore,
And a single shell, where I hear still the spell
Echoing far, as down the street
Ragged I walk. To myself I must talk,
For seldom they speak, men that I meet.'

The dialogue in *Looney* recalls that of *The Rime of the Ancient Mariner*, except that Coleridge's 'grey-beard loon' compels the wedding guest to hear his story, while the traveller in *Looney* tells his tale only after being asked to do so: 'Where have you been, what have you seen'. Here there are two voices, and men 'seldom' speak to the traveller; in *The Sea-Bell*, there is only one, for the men the traveller meets 'speak not'. Also in *The Sea-Bell*, a black cloud comes upon the traveller after he 'proudly' commands the unseen inhabitants to 'come forth all', whereas in *Looney* he 'shout[s] aloud' only after the dark cloud appears. The poems differ as well in regard to the 'sea-bell' itself: in *Looney*, the traveller returns with 'a single shell, where I hear still the spell'; in the later poem, his journey is preceded by the finding of a shell, in which he hears the 'call ringing / over endless seas', as if a summons or invitation.

Both poems describe a visit to an Otherworld lasting 'a year and a day', but only the later work includes an 'elvish' element in which those who live in the distant land are ever just out of reach. Tom Shippey has noted in *The Road to Middle-earth* that in *Looney*, the mysterious land is a vision of paradise for two stanzas before turning dark; in *The Sea-Bell*, however, menacing images – roaring breakers, 'a perilous reef', 'cliffs of stone', 'glooming caves' – occur at once, and the mood persists. 'Faërie', as Tolkien wrote, speaking of the realm of fairy-story, 'is a perilous land, and in it are pitfalls for the unwary and dungeons for the overbold. . . . [Its] very richness and strangeness tie the tongue of a traveller who would report them. And while he is there it is dangerous for him to ask too many questions, lest the gates should be shut and the keys be lost' (*On Fairy-Stories*, in *The Monsters and the Critics and Other Essays*, p. 109).

As more than one critic has said, the situation of the speaker in *Looney* and *The Sea-Bell* is common in fairy-stories: that of one who journeys to Faërie and finds himself changed. The travellers in both poems return ragged, the one in *The Sea-Bell* bent and grey, with years heavy upon his back. Also as in traditional fairy-stories, where those who try to take something from the fairy realm (or who are paid in fairy gold) find that little or nothing remains, the speaker in *Looney* counts his 'gain' as 'only withering leaves and pebbles' and 'a single shell', but at least the shell is still 'echoing far'. For the traveller in *The Sea-Bell*, having claimed power in the 'strange land' – symbolized by 'a tall wand to hold, and a flag of gold', the sceptre and sword of royalty – his 'clutching hand' retains only 'grains of sand, / and a sea-bell silent and dead'. For him, impatient to be carried away in the boat and then presumptuous in proclaiming kingship, even a distant echo of Faërie is denied: 'Never will my ear that bell hear, / never my feet that shore tread, / never again'.

In the *Bombadil* preface, Tolkien describes *The Sea-Bell* as 'certainly of hobbit origin', a late work in the time scheme of Middle-earth, with a scrawled title, *Frodos Dreme* at the head of its (fictional) manuscript. 'That', he says, 'is remarkable, and though the piece is most unlikely to have been written by Frodo himself, the title shows that it was associated with the dark and despairing dreams which visited him in March and October during his last three years.' In Book VI, Chapter 9 of *The Lord of the Rings*, and in Appendix B of that work (*The Tale of Years*), Frodo is said to fall ill on 13 March, the anniversary of his poisoning by Shelob, and on 6 October, the date he was wounded on Weathertop. 'There were certainly other traditions',

Tolkien continues, 'concerning Hobbits that were taken by the "wandering-madness"' – a rare state first mentioned in Chapter 1 of *The Hobbit* ('so many quiet lads and lasses going off into the Blue for mad adventures') – 'and if they ever returned, were afterwards queer and uncommunicable.'

'The thought of the Sea', Tolkien also says in the preface, was 'ever-present in the background of hobbit imagination'. So it was in his own: ships and gulls, cliffs and caves, wind and wave figure in many of his works. The 'glittering sand . . . / dust of pearl and jewel-grist' of *The Sea-Bell* recalls a description of Valinor, the 'Blessed Realm' of the Elves and the angelic powers, in 'The Silmarillion': 'Many jewels the Noldor gave [the Teleri], opals and diamonds and pale crystals, which they strewed upon the shores and scattered in the pools. Marvellous were the beaches of Elendë in those days' (*Morgoth's Ring* (1993), p. 43). And from the song of Eärendil in *The Lord of the Rings* (bk. II, ch. 1; see our notes for *Errantry*), 'Evereven's lofty hills / where softly silver fountains fall', referring to Valinor, are echoed in *The Sea-Bell*, where the speaker climbs 'a fountain-stair to a country fair of ever-eve'.

In a letter to Pauline Baynes, Tolkien called *The Sea-Bell* the 'poorest' of the poems he selected for the *Bombadil* collection (6 December 1961, *Letters*, p. 312), and in correspondence with Rayner Unwin he described it as 'the vaguer, more subjective and least successful piece' among those submitted (8 December 1961, A&U archive; *Reader's Guide*, p. 26); we cannot say why he thought so. In time, the work was praised by W.H. Auden, and has been the subject of much scholarship relative to the other poems in the *Bombadil* volume, most extensively by Verlyn Flieger. Among other points, Flieger has found parallels between *The Sea-Bell* (and *Looney*) and Tolkien's Old English poem of the 1920s, *Ides Ælfscýne*, in which a boy travels over the ocean to a 'far-off land, on the silver strand . . . by the dim and dreary waves', and when at last he returns home he is 'grey and alone' (translation by Tom Shippey, *The Road to Middle-earth*, p. 405; see our comments on *Shadow-Bride*). Flieger has also discussed Tolkien's late story, *Smith of Wootton Major* (1967), 'as a kind of corrective' to *The Sea-Bell*, 'sweetening the bitterness of the pain and gently balancing the loss [of Faërie] with renewed appreciation for the things of this world'. Smith, who frequently visits Faery (as it is spelled in his tale), must finally leave it and not return, but 'finds consolation in family and friends'. Like the traveller in *The Sea-Bell*, Smith 'is given to know that this Otherworld is not for him; but unlike the voyager,' he gives it up freely, if reluctantly, 'not isolated but enriched by where he has been and what he has seen' (*A Question of Time: J.R.R. Tolkien's Road to Faërie* (1997), p. 229).

In *Looney*, *moonsheen* is a variation on *moonshine*, and *frore* 'intensely cold' is the archaic past participle of *freeze*. In *The Sea-Bell*, *ruel-bone* is an obsolete word for whale-ivory, a *rill* is a small stream, *nenuphars* are water-lilies, and *gladdon-swords* are irises, also known as *flags*, with sword-shaped leaves, thus the speaker's 'flag of gold' is a yellow flag or iris. *Brocks* are badgers, and *sea-wrack* refers to seaweed which grows on the shoreline.

THE LAST SHIP

The precursor to *The Last Ship* was the poem *Firiel*, published in the *Chronicle of the Convents of the Sacred Heart*, no. 4 (1934):

> Firiel looked out at three o'clock:
>   the grey night was going;
> Far away a golden cock
>   clear and shrill was crowing.
> The trees were dark, the light was pale;
>   waking birds were cheeping;
> A wind moved cool and frail
>   through dim leaves creeping.
>
> She watched the gleam at window grow,
>   till the long light was shimmering
> On land and leaf; on grass below
>   grey dew was glimmering.
> Over the floor her white feet crept,

down the stairs they twinkled,
Through the grass they dancing stepped
all with dew besprinkled.

Her gown had jewels upon its hem,
as she ran down to the river,
And leaned upon a willow-stem,
and watched the water quiver.
A kingfisher plunged down like a stone
in a blue flash falling,
Bending reeds were softly blown,
lily-leaves were sprawling.

A sudden music to her came,
as she stood there gleaming
With free hair in the morning's flame
on her shoulders streaming.
Flutes there were, and harps were wrung,
and there was sound of singing
Like wind-voices keen and young
in green leaves swinging.

A boat with golden beak and oar
and timbers white came gliding;

Swans went sailing on before,
    her swift course guiding.
Fair folk out of Elvenland
    robed in white were rowing,
And three with crowns she saw there stand
    with bright hair flowing.

They sang their song, while minstrels played
    on harp and flute slowly
Like sea heard in a green glade
    under mountains holy.
The beak was turned, the boat drew nigh
    with elven-treasure laden,
'Firiel! Come aboard!' they cry,
    'O fair earth-maiden!'

'O whither go ye, Elvenfolk,
    down the waters gliding?
To the twilight under beech and oak
    in the green forest hiding?
To foam that falls upon the shore
    and the white gulls crying?
To Northern isles grey and frore
    on strong swans flying?'

'Nay! Out and onward, far away
    past oak and elm and willow,
Leaving western havens grey,
    cleaving the green billow,
We go back to Elvenhome
    beyond the last mountains,
Whose feet are in the outer foam
    of the world's deep fountains.

In Elvenhome a clear bell
    is in white tower shaking!
To wood and water say farewell,
    the long road taking!
Here grass fades and leaves fall
    and sun and moon wither;
And to few comes the far call
    that bids them journey hither.'

Firiel looked from the river-bank,
    one step daring;
And then her heart misgave and shrank,
    and she halted staring.
Higher climbed the round sun,
    and the dew was drying;

Faint faded, one by one,
   their far voices crying.

No jewels bright her gown bore,
   as she walked back from the water,
Under roof and dark door,
   earth's fair daughter.
At eight o'clock in green and white,
   with long hair braided,
She tripped down, leaving night
   and a vision faded.

Up climbed the round sun,
   and the world was busy,
In and out, walk and run,
   like an anthill dizzy.
Inside the house were feet
   going pitter-patter;
Brooms, dusters, mats to beat,
   pails, and dishes clatter.

Breakfast was on table laid;
   there were voices loud and merry;
There was jam, honey, marmalade,

milk and fruit, and berry.
Of this and that people spoke,
jest, work, and money,
Shooting bird, and felling oak,
and 'please, pass the honey!'

Tolkien wrote *Firiel* in the early 1930s, and submitted it to a journal published by an order of Roman Catholic nuns. He was in close contact with their Oxford convent (established 1929): his daughter, Priscilla, attended children's parties there in the summer, and at Christmas while her father provided entertainment.

The name *Firiel* (in the 1934 poem printed without an accent) means 'mortal woman' in Tolkien's invented 'High-Elvish' language, and is found several times in his 'Silmarillion' mythology. In the *Bombadil* preface, he expands its use as the name also of 'a princess of Gondor, through whom Aragorn [in *The Lord of the Rings*] claimed descent from the Southern line', and of 'a daughter of Elanor, daughter of Sam [Gamgee], but her name, if connected with the rhyme, must be derived from it'. With *The Man in the Moon Came Down Too Soon* (see above), *The Last Ship* is said to 'be derived ultimately from Gondor', with its 'rivers running into the Sea', and only a re-handling 'of Southern matter, though this may have reached Bilbo by way of [the Elvish refuge of] Rivendell'.

Firiel and *The Last Ship* are alike in many respects. A mortal woman (the unnamed illustrator of the 1934 poem depicted her as a child) leaves her home in the early morning, her feet *twinkling* (moving lightly and rapidly) down the stair and dancing in the grass. She sees a company of elves, '*fair folk* out of Elvenland' (applying a traditional term for elves or fairies), pass by on the water, leaving western *havens* (harbours). They invite her to join them, to sail to 'Elvenhome'. She dares to take one step forward, but no further. At last, she returns home to family or work. In *Firiel*, however, the elves cry simply for the 'fair earth-maiden' to come aboard; in *The Last Ship*, the invitation is made with urgency: they have 'heard the far call' to sail for Elvenhome, and does she hear it too? Their ship may bear only one more; Fíriel's 'days are speeding' – her mortality is swiftly passing – and for the 'Earth-maiden elven-fair' it is the 'last call': there will be no more elven-boats passing by.

In *Firiel*, at the moment of truth 'her heart misgave and shrank, / and she halted staring', until the boat has moved on and the elves' voices are lost in the distance; she is not led into temptation. In contrast, in *The Last*

Ship Fíriel's feet sink 'deep in clay'. Reminded of her mortality, she accepts her fate: she 'cannot' go with the immortal elves, for although 'elven-fair', she was 'born Earth's daughter'. In *Firiel,* she walks back from the water, 'leaving night / and a vision faded' in favour of life in a busy household: 'Brooms, dusters, mats to beat, / pails, and dishes clatter'. But the dénouement is cheerful, with 'voices loud and merry' and 'please, pass the honey!' *The Last Ship* ends instead on a note of profound sadness, with Fíriel dressed in 'russet brown' (in the earlier version, in green and white), 'under the house-shadow', and the sunlight and the elves' song both 'faded'.

The 'jewels' upon the gown's hem are evidently to be taken as dew, for after a time 'no jewels bright her gown bore' – they have evaporated (in the 1934 poem 'the dew was drying' as the sun climbed) – though they may also be symbolic of the promise of the fresh morning, compared with the return of Firiel/Fíriel 'under roof and dark door'. In any event, they are part of the imagery of nature Tolkien establishes, as the world of mortals, before introducing the other-worldly 'boat with golden *beak* [a projection at the prow] and oar / and timbers white'. The swans 'sailing on before' recall those in 'The Silmarillion' which guide the ships of the Teleri.

As a gloss to *Elvenland*, Tolkien notes in the preface that 'in the Langstrand and Dol Amroth [both in the southern part of Gondor] there were many traditions of the ancient Elvish dwellings, and of the haven at the mouth of the Morthond from which "westward ships" had sailed as far back as the fall of Eregion in the Second Age'. (Compare also Sam's sad comment in *The Lord of the Rings*, Book I, Chapter 2: 'They are sailing, sailing, sailing over the Sea, they are going into the West and leaving us'.) In the poems, 'Elvenland' stands in contrast to the elves' destination, *Elvenhome*, which in the context of Tolkien's mythology usually refers to the land of Aman in the far West of the world (as opposed to elven-lands in Middle-earth), and in later stories was forbidden to mortals. In *Firiel*, Elvenhome is to be found 'beyond the last mountains, / Whose feet are in the outer foam / of the world's deep fountains', a description which strongly evokes Tolkien's mythology, with Valinor behind the walls of the Pelóri, the Mountains of Aman. In *The Last Ship*, the elves dare 'the seas of shadow' on 'the last road' – the sea-path 'filled with shadows and bewilderment' (*The Silmarillion*, p. 102) – to return to 'where the White Tree is growing', presumably (in the mythology) Galathilion, the White Tree of Tirion, and where 'the Star shines upon the foam', presumably a reference to Eärendil, the celestial mariner. In both poems, the elves hear 'a clear bell' in a white, or high, tower, the call that bids them journey; there are several white (or silver) towers in 'The Silmarillion', among them the high Tower of Ingwë with its silver lamp, and the white tower of Elwing on the edge of the Sundering Seas.

In the earlier poem, Firiel hails the mariners explicitly as 'Elvenfolk', but in *The Last Ship* they are 'boatmen fair' – though probably Tolkien intended no difference in meaning. The destination Firiel/Fíriel describes in her question to them, variously to 'twilight', 'under beech and oak' or 'to secret lair', in the green (or great) forest 'hiding', to 'Northern isles grey and *frore*' (frozen) and 'shores of stone', recalls in a general fashion the landscape of Northern myth and legend.

In *The Last Ship*, Firiel's brown *smock* is an overgarment to protect her clothing as she works. The *Seven Rivers* of the final stanza are identified in the preface as the Lefnui, Morthond–Kiril–Ringló, Gilrain–Serni, and Anduin. The hyphenated rivers join before they reach the sea.

Gallery

These pages by J.R.R. Tolkien are three of the earliest (*c.* 1931) examples of his 'Elvish' alphabet which evolved into the *tengwar* of *The Lord of the Rings*. Although in different calligraphic styles, they use the same system of letter values for transcription. The first two are excerpts from the earlier version of *The Adventures of Tom Bombadil*, while the third is from *Errantry*; all vary slightly from the poems as published. Reproductions of these pages first appeared, in colour, in *The Silmarillion Calendar* 1978, and later in *Pictures by J.R.R. Tolkien* (1979). See further, Tolkien, *The Qenya Alphabet* (2012).

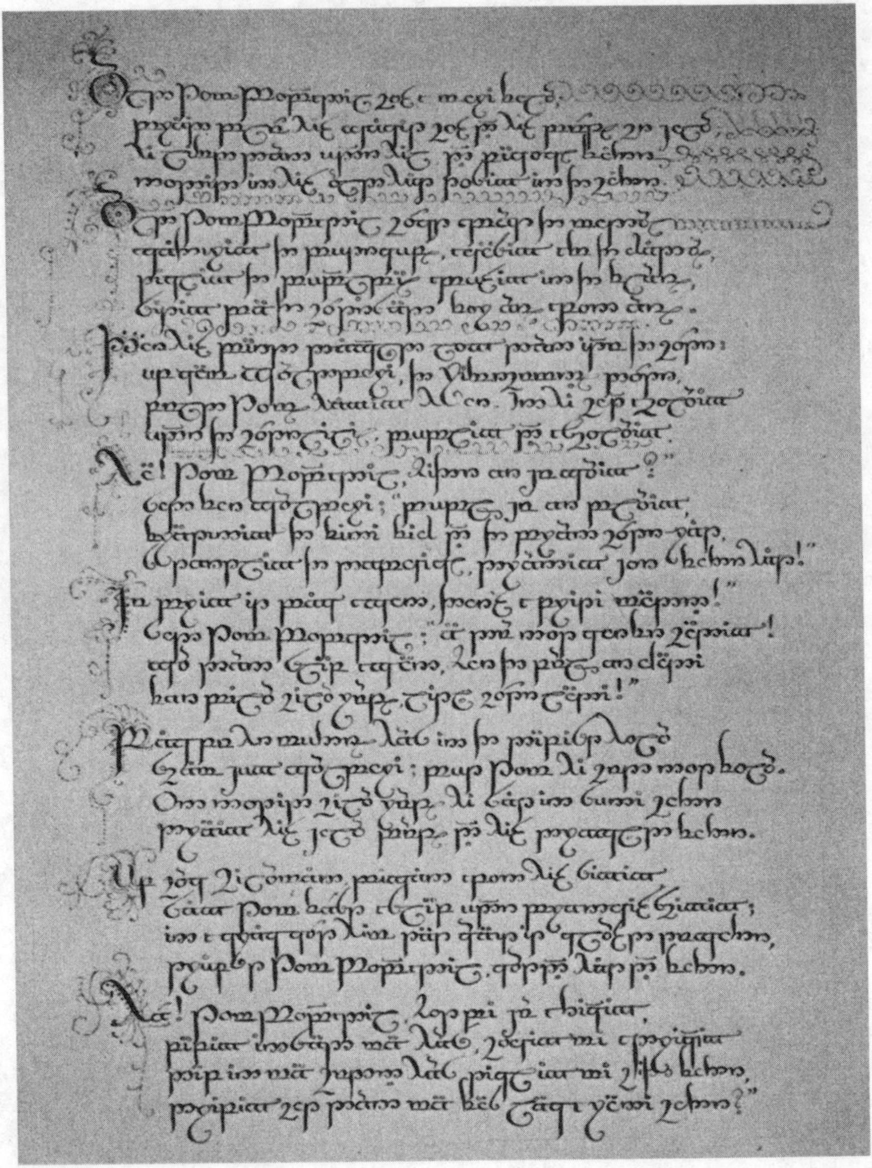

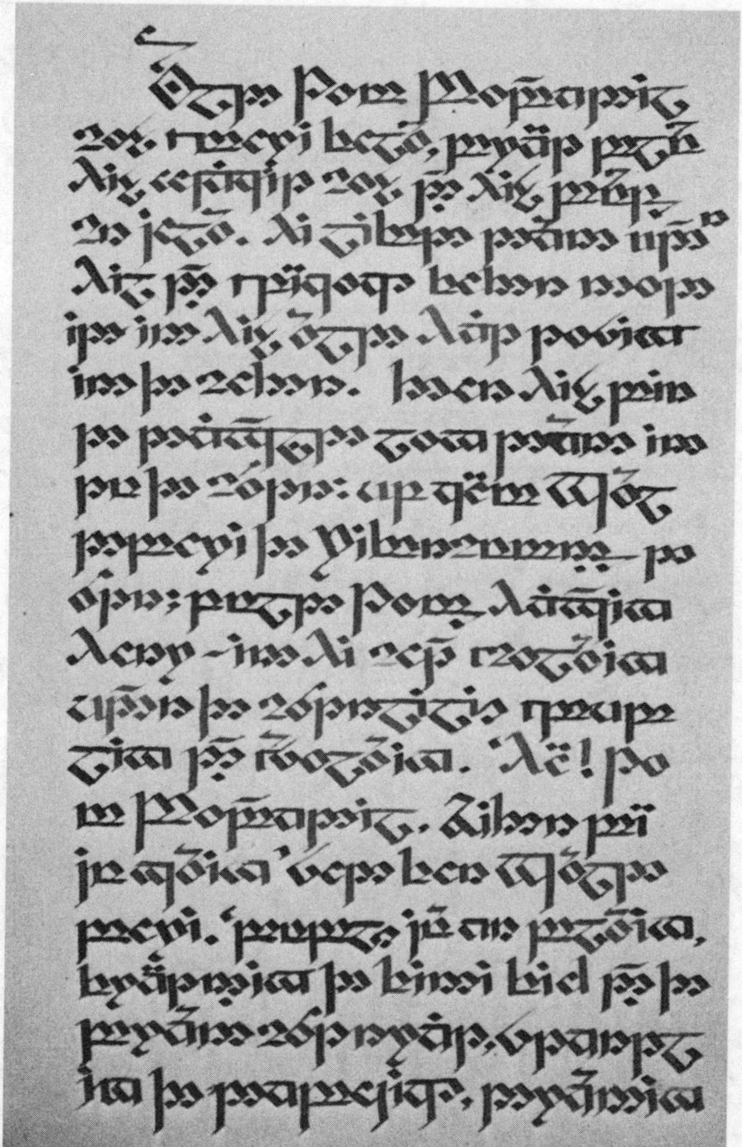

Appendix

Overleaf is an illustration of Old Man Willow by Pauline Baynes,
made for Tolkien's *Poems and Stories* (1981). Another illustration
from this collection, of Tom Bombadil, appears at the end of the
present volume

I. *Tom Bombadil: A Prose Fragment*

Among the Tolkien papers in the Bodleian Library, Oxford, and partly printed in Humphrey Carpenter's *Biography*, is a fragment of a prose tale, entitled *Tom Bombadil*, written probably in the 1920s. Unfortunately, Tolkien ceased to write, or the surviving manuscript fails, after only three paragraphs:

> It happened in the days of King Bonhedig, before the wild men came hither out of Ond, or the dark men out of Euskadi, or the fair haired warriors with long iron swords across the narrow water; in fact before any one ever mentioned in fantastic history or sober legend had yet arrived in Britain (as it was called in those days), a long time ago, and before the most far-reaching prophecies, of which there was a multitude, had even glimpsed Arthur in the distant and incredible future.
>
> Nonetheless things already happened here and the island was full enough of peoples and other inhab-itants, and had already suffered many invasions and

changed (as since) everything but its name several times over. King Bonhedig sat upon the throne of the Kingdom of Bon [*added:* & Barroc] which stretched for many miles on either side of the Tames as they called the chief river of the South. There we will leave him, for he concerns us only as a convenient method of dating. He reigned for fifty years only, so you will not be far out in whatever part of his reign you place these events.

Tombombadil [*sic*] was the name of one [of] the oldest inhabitants of the kingdom; but he was a hale and hearty fellow. Four foot high in his boots he was, and three foot broad; his beard went below his knees; his eyes were keen and bright, and his voice deep and melodious. He wore a tall hat with a blue feather[;] his jacket was blue, and his boots were yellow.

Bonhedig (*Bonheddig*) is Welsh for 'noble'. *Ond* is an ancient word for 'stone', almost the lone survivor of the language that preceded the Celts and the Germanic invaders of Britain; Tolkien incorporated it in 'Elvish' words such as *Gondor* 'stone-land'. *Euskadi* is the Basque country in northern Spain. The 'narrow water' is presumably the English Channel. The name *Barroc* – if this is the correct reading; in the manuscript the word is smudged – may be meant to refer to the forest (or possibly hill), variously spelled, thought to be a source element for *Berkshire*, the name of a county which borders on the river Thames (here 'Tames').

II. *Once upon a Time* and *An Evening in Tavrobel*

In addition to *The Adventures of Tom Bombadil* and *Bombadil Goes Boating* in *The Adventures of Tom Bombadil and Other Verses from the Red Book*, Tolkien published a third poem featuring Goldberry and Tom Bombadil, *Once upon a Time*, in a collection of new poetry and stories, *Winter's Tales for Children 1*, edited by Caroline Hillier (1965):

> Once upon a day on the fields of May
> there was snow in summer where the blossom lay;
> the buttercups tall sent up their light
> in a steam of gold, and wide and white
> there opened in the green grass-skies
> the earth-stars with their steady eyes
> watching the Sun climb up and down.
> Goldberry was there with a wild-rose crown,
> Goldberry was there in a lady-smock
> blowing away a dandelion clock,

stooping over a lily-pool
and twiddling the water green and cool
to see it sparkle round her hand:
once upon a time in elvish land.

Once upon a night in the cockshut light
the grass was grey but the dew was white;
shadows were dark, and the Sun was gone,
the earth-stars shut, but the high stars shone,
one to another winking their eyes
as they waited for the Moon to rise.
Up he came, and on leaf and grass
his white beams turned to twinkling glass,
and silver dripped from stem and stalk
down to where the lintips walk
through the grass-forests gathering dew.
Tom was there without boot or shoe,
with moonshine wetting his big brown toes:
once upon a time, the story goes.

Once upon a moon on the brink of June
a-dewing the lintips went too soon.
Tom stopped and listened, and down he knelt:
'Ha! little lads! So it was you I smelt?
What a mousy smell! Well, the dew is sweet,

So drink it up, but mind my feet!'
The lintips laughed and stole away,
but old Tom said: 'I wish they'd stay!
The only things that won't talk to me,
say what they do or what they be.
I wonder what they have got to hide?
Down from the Moon maybe they slide,
or come in star-winks, I don't know':
Once upon a time and long ago.

Invited in 1964 to contribute to the first of a series
of anthologies for children, Tolkien submitted three
poems, of which two were published: *Once upon a
Time*, and a revised version of *The Dragon's Visit* (see
our introduction). He may have composed *Once upon
a Time* for this purpose, or not long before; at least,
the poem seems to have been written after 1962, since
there is no mention in correspondence of Tolkien con-
sidering it for the *Bombadil* collection.

Once upon a Time stands apart from the other two
'Tom Bombadil' poems also for other reasons. In those
works (and in *The Lord of the Rings*), Tom is able to
communicate with all living creatures, but here the
lintips are 'the only things that won't talk to me'. Here
too, unlike the other poems to feature them, *Once upon*

a Time is concerned less with the adventures of Tom and Goldberry than with the natural world, as a riot of flowers by day gives way to the silent, night-time beauty of dew upon leaf and grass. Finally, Tom is named only as 'Tom', left to be identified by the reader with Tom Bombadil from Tolkien's other writings, in particular because Goldberry is named in the same work.

Although 'snow in summer' in the first stanza could refer to the wildflower Summer snowflake, it seems more likely that the 'snow' is made of the fallen white blossoms of the Hawthorn, also known as May or Mayblossom ('the fields of May'), from the typical month of its flowering. The 'buttercups tall' with a 'steam of gold' are presumably a variety of *Ranunculus*. The 'earth-stars' 'opened in the green grass-skies' – that is, in a green landscape echoing the heavens – may be one of the common fungi of the family *Geastraceae*, commonly called 'earth-stars' for their star-like form when opened; Kris Swank in *Tolkien Studies* (2013), however, wonders if Tolkien meant the common daisy, which opens in the sun (the 'day's eye') and closes at night, a 'star of earth' as the Sun is a star of the sky. Goldberry's 'lady-smock' may be a protective overgarment – Tolkien uses *smock* in this sense elsewhere in his poems – but *lady-smock* is also a kind of wildflower.

Finally, *dandelion clock* refers to the children's game of blowing away dandelion seeds and counting the number of puffs, which is supposed to tell the time.

In the second stanza, Tolkien follows a folk-belief that dew is formed by the moon, its light 'turned to twinkling glass, / and silver'. Here he also introduces the 'lintips', which despite much effort by scholars remain a mystery. They are small enough to 'walk / through the grass-forests', so perhaps (as Douglas A. Anderson, Kris Swank, and others have suggested) a kind of mouse or vole, or even an insect; and they are nocturnal, coming out in 'the *cockshut light*' (at twilight). A stronger possibility, as it seems to us, proposed in an unpublished paper by Rhona Beare, is that the lintips are the same tiny spirits of which Tolkien wrote in *An Evening in Tavrobel*, a poem of 1924 (published in *Leeds University Verse 1914–24*) which includes so many similarities with *Once upon a Time* that the latter poem could be seen as a development of the former:

'Tis the time when May first looks toward June,
With almond-scented hawthorn strewn.
The tremulous day at last has run
Down the gold stairways of the Sun,
Who brimmed the buttercups with light

Like a clear wine she spillèd bright;
And gleaming spirits there did dance
And sip those goblets' radiance.

Now wane they all; now comes the moon;
Like crystal are the dewdrops strewn
Beneath the eve, and twinkling gems
Are hung on the leaves and slender stems.
Now in the grass lies many a pool,
Infinitesimal and cool,
Where tiny faces peer and laugh
At glassy fragments of the stars
About them mirrored, or from jars
Of unimagined frailty quaff
This essence of the plenilune,
Thirsty, perchance, from dancing all the noon.

Tavrobel figures in the early conception of Tolkien's mythology, as the home of fairies, or elves; but this connection of the poem to 'The Silmarillion' does not appear to extend beyond its title.

In the end, like the creatures in *The Mewlips*, the lintips cannot be defined or, beyond a point, described, and absent any further explanation by Tolkien, no one can say 'what they do or what they be'. Nor has a satisfactory source been agreed for the name *lintips*, in English or in one of Tolkien's invented languages (a search inspired by the words 'elvish land' at the end of the first stanza). It may be that he adopted *lintips* for no more reason than it gave him pleasure, just as he once was pleased (as he wrote in his essay *A Secret Vice*, on the invention of private languages) to combine the sound of *lint* with the meaning 'quick, clever, nimble' (*The Monsters and the Critics and Other Essays*, p. 205).

BIBLIOGRAPHY

Previously published poems by Tolkien printed or quoted, excepting those in *The Adventures of Tom Bombadil and Other Verses from the Red Book* (1962), were taken from the following sources:

The Adventures of Tom Bombadil. Oxford Magazine (Oxford) 52, no. 13 (15 February 1934), pp. 464–5.

The Cat and the Fiddle. Yorkshire Poetry (Leeds) 2, no. 19 (October–November 1924), pp. 1–3.

Errantry. Oxford Magazine (Oxford) 52, no. 5 (9 November 1933), p. 180.

An Evening in Tavrobel. Leeds University Verse 1914–24. Comp. and ed. the English School Association. Leeds: At the Swan Press, 1924. p. 56.

Fastitocalon. Stapeldon Magazine (Exeter College, Oxford) 7, no. 40 (June 1927), pp. 123–5.

Firiel. Chronicle of the Convents of the Sacred Heart (Roehampton), no. 4 (1934), pp. 30–2.

Iumbo, or ye Kinde of ye Oliphaunt. Stapeldon Magazine

(Exeter College, Oxford) 7, no. 40 (June 1927), pp. 125–7.

Iúmonna Gold Galdre Bewunden. The Gryphon (Leeds), new series 4, no. 4 (January 1923), p. 130.

Iúmonna Gold Galdre Bewunden. Oxford Magazine (Oxford) 55, no. 15 (4 March 1937), p. 473.

Knocking at the Door. Oxford Magazine (Oxford) 55, no. 13 (18 February 1937), p. 403.

Looney. Oxford Magazine (Oxford) 52, no. 9 (18 January 1934), p. 340.

Once upon a Time. Winter's Tales for Children 1. Ed. Caroline Hillier. Illustrated by Hugh Marshall. London: Macmillan; New York: St Martin's Press, 1965. pp. 44–5.

Princess Ní. Leeds University Verse 1914–24. Comp. and ed. the English School Association. Leeds: Swan Press, 1924. p. 58.

The Root of the Boot. Songs for the Philologists. London: Privately printed in the Department of English at University College, 1936. pp. 20–1.

The Shadow Man. The 'Annual' of Our Lady's School, Abingdon, no. 12 (1936), p. 9.

Why the Man in the Moon Came Down Too Soon. A Northern Venture: Verses by Members of the Leeds University English School Association. Leeds: Swan Press, 1923. pp. 17–19.

Bombadil Goes Boating, *Perry-the-Winkle*, and *Cat* had no earlier published versions. *The Bumpus*, predecessor of *Perry-the-Winkle*, has been transcribed from a manuscript provided by Christopher Tolkien. We have also referred to manuscript and typescript versions of *Knocking at the Door* (later *The Mewlips*) furnished by Christopher Tolkien, to the Tolkien archive in the Bodleian Library, Oxford, and to the Tolkien–George Allen & Unwin archive of correspondence now held by HarperCollins. When part of a quotation from the Allen & Unwin archive has been published already in *Letters of J.R.R. Tolkien* or *The J.R.R. Tolkien Companion and Guide*, we have cited the latter as well. Other works consulted include:

Anderson, Douglas A. 'The Mystery of Lintips'. *Tolkien and Fantasy* (blog), 22 July 2013. http://tolkienandfantasy. blogspot.com/2013/07/the-mystery-of-lintips.html.

Beare, Rhona. 'The Trumpets of Dawn'. Typescript of unpublished lecture.

Carpenter, Humphrey. *J.R.R. Tolkien: A Biography*. London: George Allen & Unwin, 1977.

Christie's. *20th Century Books and Manuscripts*. Auction catalogue. London (St James's), 2 December 2003.

Clark, Willene B. *A Medieval Book of Beasts: The Second-Family Bestiary*. Woodbridge, Suffolk: Boydell Press, 2006.

Coward, T.A. *The Birds of the British Isles and Their Eggs.* 5th edn. London: Frederick Warne, 1936.

Derrick, Christopher. 'From an Antique Land'. *The Tablet,* 15 December 1962, p. 1227.

Duggan, Alfred. 'Middle Earth Verse'. *Times Literary Supplement,* 23 November 1962, p. 892.

Eilmann, Julian, and Allan Turner. *Tolkien's Poetry.* Zurich: Walking Tree Publishers, 2013. Three of the included essays are concerned variously with *Errantry, The Hoard, The Man in the Moon Came Down Too Soon,* and *The Sea-Bell.*

Ekwall, Eilert. *The Concise Oxford Dictionary of English Place-names.* 4th edn. Oxford: Clarendon Press, 1960.

Fisher, Jason. 'The Origins of Tolkien's "Errantry"' (parts 1 and 2). *Lingwë: Musings of a Fish* (blog), 25 September and 1 October 2008. http://lingwe.blogspot.com/2008/09/origins-of-tolkiens-errantry-part-1.html, http://lingwe.blogspot.com/2008/10/origins-of-tolkiens-errantry-part-2.html.

Flieger, Verlyn. *A Question of Time: J.R.R. Tolkien's Road to Faërie.* Kent, Ohio: Kent State University Press, 1997.

—— *Splintered Light: Logos and Language in Tolkien's World.* Rev. edn. Kent, Ohio: Kent State University Press, 2002.

Gilliver, Peter M., Jeremy Marshall, and Edmund Weiner. *The Ring of Words: Tolkien and the* Oxford English Dictionary. Oxford: Oxford University Press, 2006.

Hammond, Wayne G. *J.R.R. Tolkien: A Descriptive Bibliography*. With the assistance of Douglas A. Anderson. Winchester: St Paul's Bibliographies; New Castle, Delaware: Oak Knoll Books, 1993.

—— and Christina Scull. *J.R.R. Tolkien: Artist and Illustrator*. London: HarperCollins, 1995.

—— *The Lord of the Rings: A Reader's Companion*. London: HarperCollins, 2005.

Helms, Randel. *Tolkien's World*. Boston: Houghton Mifflin, 1974.

Hiley, Margaret, and Frank Weinreich, eds. *Tolkien's Shorter Works: Proceedings of the 4th Seminar of the Deutsche Tolkien Gesellschaft & Walking Tree Publishers Decennial Conference*. Zurich: Walking Tree Publishers, 2008. Several of the included essays are concerned with poems from the *Bombadil* volume, especially *The Sea-Bell*.

Honegger, Thomas. 'The Man in the Moon: Structural Depth in Tolkien'. In *Root and Branch: Approaches towards Understanding Tolkien*. Ed. Thomas Honegger. Zurich: Walking Tree Publishers, 1999. pp. 9–76.

Johnston, George Burke. 'The Poetry of J.R.R. Tolkien'. *Mankato State University Studies* 2, no. 1 (February 1967), pp. 63–75.

Kocher, Paul H. *Master of Middle-earth: The Fiction of J.R.R. Tolkien*. Boston: Houghton Mifflin, 1972.

MacDonald, George. *At the Back of the North Wind*. 1870; rpt. London: J.M. Dent & Sons, 1956.

MacKillop, James. *Dictionary of Celtic Mythology*. Oxford: Oxford University Press, 1998.

O'Donaghue, Denis. *Lives and Legends of Saint Brendan the Voyager*. Felinfach: Llanerch Publishers, 1994. Facsimile of the edn. first published at Dublin, 1893.

Opie, Iona, and Peter Opie. *The Lore and Language of Schoolchildren*. Oxford: Oxford University Press, 1959.

—— *The Oxford Dictionary of Nursery Rhymes*. New edn. Oxford: Oxford University Press, 1997.

Rateliff, John D. *The History of The Hobbit*. London: HarperCollins, 2007. 2 vols.

—— 'J.R.R. Tolkien: Sir Topas Revisited'. *Notes and Queries* 29, no. 4 (August 1982), p. 348.

—— 'The New Arrival: *Winter's Tales for Children*'. *Sacnoth's Scriptorium* (blog), 13 July 2009. http://sacnoths. blogspot.com/2009/07/new-arrival-winters-tales-for-children.html.

Scull, Christina. 'Tom Bombadil and *The Lord of the Rings*'. *Leaves from the Tree: J.R.R. Tolkien's Shorter Fiction*. London: Tolkien Society, 1991. pp. 73–7.

—— and Wayne G. Hammond. *The J.R.R. Tolkien Companion and Guide*. London: HarperCollins, 2006. 2 vols.: *Chronology, Reader's Guide*.

Shippey, Tom. *The Road to Middle-earth*. Rev. and expanded edn. London: HarperCollins, 2005.

—— 'The Versions of "The Hoard"'. *Roots and Branches:*

Selected Papers on Tolkien. Zollikofen: Walking Tree Publishers, 2007. pp. 341–9.

Michael Silverman. *Manuscripts, Autograph Letters & Historical Documents: Recent Acquisitions*. London, 1995.

Simpson, Jacqueline, and Steve Roud. *A Dictionary of English Folklore*. Oxford: Oxford University Press, 2000.

Smith, A.H. *English Place-name Elements*. Cambridge: Cambridge University Press, 1956. 2 vols.

Sotheby's. *English Literature and English History*. Auction catalogue. London, 6–7 December 1984.

Swank, Kris. 'Tom Bombadil's Last Song: Tolkien's "Once upon a Time"'. *Tolkien Studies* 10 (2013), pp. 185–97.

Thwaite, Anthony. 'Hobbitry'. *The Listener*, 22 November 1962, p. 831.

Tolkien, J.R.R. *The Adventures of Tom Bombadil and Other Verses from the Red Book*. London: George Allen & Unwin, 1962. The second printing, with revised order of poems, was also published in 1962.

—— *The Annotated Hobbit*. Rev. and expanded edn. Annotated by Douglas A. Anderson. Boston: Houghton Mifflin, 2002.

—— *Beowulf and the Critics*. Rev. 2nd edn. Ed. Michael D.C. Drout. Tempe, Arizona: Arizona Center for Medieval and Renaissance Studies, 2011.

—— *The Book of Lost Tales, Part One*. Ed. Christopher Tolkien. London: George Allen & Unwin, 1983.

—— *Farmer Giles of Ham*. London: George Allen & Unwin, 1949.

—— *The J.R.R. Tolkien Audio Collection*. London: HarperCollins, 2001.

——. *J.R.R. Tolkien Reads and Sings His The Hobbit and The Fellowship of the Ring*. New York: Caedmon Records, 1975.

—— *J.R.R. Tolkien Reads and Sings His The Lord of the Rings: The Two Towers/The Return of the King*. New York: Caedmon Records, 1975.

—— *The Lays of Beleriand*. Ed. Christopher Tolkien. London: George Allen & Unwin, 1985.

—— *The Legend of Sigurd and Gudrún*. Ed. Christopher Tolkien. London: HarperCollins, 2009.

—— *Letters from Father Christmas*. Ed. Baillie Tolkien. London: HarperCollins, 1999.

—— *Letters of J.R.R. Tolkien*. Ed. Humphrey Carpenter, with the assistance of Christopher Tolkien. London: HarperCollins, 2000.

—— *The Lord of the Rings*. 50th anniversary edn. London: HarperCollins, 2005.

—— *The Lost Road and Other Writings: Language and Legend before 'The Lord of the Rings'*. Ed. Christopher Tolkien. London: Unwin Hyman, 1987.

—— *The Monsters and the Critics and Other Essays*. Ed. Christopher Tolkien. London: George Allen & Unwin, 1983. Includes *On Fairy-Stories* and *A Secret Vice*, etc.

—— *Morgoth's Ring: The Later Silmarillion, Part One: The Legends of Aman.* Ed. Christopher Tolkien. London: HarperCollins, 1993.

—— *Pictures by J.R.R. Tolkien.* Foreword and notes by Christopher Tolkien. London: George Allen & Unwin, 1979.

—— *Poems and Songs of Middle Earth.* New York: Caedmon Records, 1967. Recording of readings by Tolkien from the *Bombadil* collection, and of the song cycle *The Road Goes Ever On* by Donald Swann, including *Errantry*.

—— *Poems and Stories.* Illustrated by Pauline Baynes. London: George Allen & Unwin, 1980.

—— *The Qenya Alphabet.* Ed. Arden R. Smith. *Parma Eldalamberon* 20. Mountain View, California: Parma Eldalamberon, 2012. Includes analysis of excerpts from *The Adventures of Tom Bombadil* and *Errantry* written in an 'Elvish' script.

—— *The Return of the Shadow: The History of The Lord of the Rings, Part One.* Ed. Christopher Tolkien. London: Unwin Hyman, 1988.

—— *The Rivers and Beacon-hills of Gondor.* Ed. Carl F. Hostetter, with additional commentary by Christopher Tolkien. *Vinyar Tengwar* 42 (July 2001), pp. 5–34.

—— *The Road Goes Ever On: A Song Cycle.* Music by Donald Swann. Boston: Houghton Mifflin, 1967.

—— *Roverandom.* Ed. Christina Scull and Wayne G. Hammond. London: HarperCollins, 1998.

—— *A Secret Vice*. In *The Monsters and the Critics and Other Essays*. Ed. Christopher Tolkien. London: George Allen & Unwin, 1983. pp. 198–223.

—— *The Shaping of Middle-earth: The Quenta, the Ambarkanta and the Annals*. Ed. Christopher Tolkien. London: George Allen & Unwin, 1986.

—— *The Silmarillion*. Ed. Christopher Tolkien. London: George Allen & Unwin, 1977.

—— *Tales from the Perilous Realm*. London: HarperCollins, 1997.

—— *The Treason of Isengard*. Ed. Christopher Tolkien. London: Unwin Hyman, 1989.

—— *Unfinished Tales of Númenor and Middle-earth*. Ed. Christopher Tolkien. London: George Allen & Unwin, 1980.

White, T.H. *The Bestiary: A Book of Beasts*. New York: Capricorn Books, 1960.